THE HEIR TO THE EMERALD CROWN

L.B. DIVINE

First paperback edition March 2024

IBSN: 979-8-9873957-5-2

E-BOOK IBSN: 979-8-9873957-4-5

Hardcover Art by @its_minuitae

Paperback Cover by @nox.benedicta.art

Map by @centuar.maps

Developmental and Copy Editing by @kmortonedits

Proofreading by Poisoned Ink Press LLC

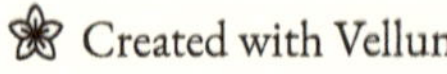 Created with Vellum

Content Warning: This book depicts loss, trauma, anxiety, death of a loved one, emotional abuse, and sacrifice. If any of these warnings could be triggering for you, please proceed with care.

N
S
E
W
Caves of Mercy
Kingdom of Criostal
River of Eamon
River of Daileen
Morganita
Haversin
Forest of Just
Kingdom of Teine
Alexandriti
Mt. Giamhnait
The Isle

CHARACTER GUIDE

Orlaith (or-la) Kearan (keer-awn) — she/her
Cathal (caw-hal) Ambronisa (am-bro-nee-sah) — he/him
Darragh (dar-rah) Ambronisa (am-bro-nee-sah) — he/him
King Ahren (air-ren) — he/him
Dealla (deal-la) Rayavarus (ra-yah-var-us) —she/her
Eowen (e-oh-when) — she/her
Eithne (et-na) — she/her
Alby (al-bee) — they/them
Aoife (ee-fa) Tavish (ta-fish) — she/her
Belanor (bell-ah-nor) — he/him
Fon (f-on) — they/them
Folen (fall-en) — he/him

PROLOGUE

The corner of the continent crackled with a dark power so rich in venom that the wind sizzled, and the ground shook with madness. Humans, elves, and creatures alike would quake in the wake of such unhinged darkness. Hissing and whispering mixed together like fire and ice, smoke rising from their lips as a vindication for their years of silence. The wraiths of death had arrived, and they would not leave until they had what they sought.

But what were they looking for?

Seated beyond the Caves of Mercy, they laid in an eternal wake. They did not sleep. They did not eat. They only waited to receive word. Dark gloved hands danced through the shadows as they reached for their long swords. Crystals, once bright and full of light, barely glistened beneath the haze of the ashy world on the hilt of the blades. With shadowed hands, they picked up their weapons and silently pledged to be in unison on this.

This destruction.

The language spoken among the creatures was not one for the common tongue, for the Gods themselves of Just and Mercy may be the only creatures to receive and understand such verbiage. Whispering among themselves as they moved toward the border of the Kingdom of Criostal, the wraiths unsheathed their swords with a heinous thrumming. Behind them, the nameless creatures roared in pleasure, their ears accustomed to such a foul sound.

They held their weapons between their horrifyingly beautiful hands as they silently dreamed of the Emerald Crown and stepped through the mist in their descent to take it.

They would take it for themselves, of course.

Eighteen Years Ago

LIGHT BLASTED through the chambers of the Criostal castle with vengeance—a payment for the eternal darkness which had harbored there decades before. Black walls danced with the shadows that remained a permanent reminder of the darkness that dwelled on their doorstep: the Kingdom of Teine. Criostal had dawned a new day, one which they would demand retribution from for years to come. The crown had been stolen this morning, when the king and queen had been most vulnerable.

And the king was more vulnerable than ever.

He had made deals, promised creatures anything, to save his wife. But the Gods could only intervene so much, could only prevent so much life from being taken, and as a result, she was not saved. Cursing himself, the king thought back to the wolven, the deal he had tried to strike the night before.

Save the queen, save his daughter, and the rest of the Isle could go to hell.

Shaking his head, he ran his long fingers over his face in dismay. He had tried everything, given everything, and his family still suffered at the hands of death's mercy.

If this was mercy, he did not wish to know what justification was. The deal had not been struck, but he knew in his heart that something had been taken from him. Beyond the crown.

The babe that laid in the crib did not stir, despite the immense power which flowed from her chest. She was the opposite of all things that this castle was—she was the light of the world, the silencer of the darkness. Cooing before turning her head to the side, she kicked her feet ever so slightly—the only signal to her father that she lived, while her mother did not.

"My sweet golden princess," her father whispered, his voice thick among the grief that clouded his soul. Reaching out a hand, he softly rubbed the top of her head. Her icy blonde hair was like the first snowfall of winter, so delicate and warm for being so cold. "The world is yours now, my Orlaith."

Leaning forward, her father placed a kiss atop her head. The babe did not stir beyond the movements she had already been making. Smiling down at her, her father breathed in through his nose and out through his mouth with a deep sigh. He welcomed the broken heart that sang at the sight of his beautiful child. She was to be his first and only heir, and at the cost of the kingdom's most prized relic and his wife's life, she had made her journey into this world.

Something told the King of Criostal that this would not be her only moment of surprise in life, that she was to be full of that same commanding presence that had brought her into the castle.

For six days her father had sat atop the throne, waiting for an answer from the wet nurses about the queen's fate. For six mornings—and six nights—he had stood proud, putting on a face of resilience for all of the kingdom to see. He had put on a face, despite what he already knew, that the Emerald Crown was gone, and with it, the powers of his family would fade.

This very morning, when word had reached him about the fate of his beloved, he could be strong no more. Collapsing to the floor in hysterical sobs, he had dashed to the nursery to covet the last remaining item of his queen. Of his wife.

And then the king had decided to lie down next to her body, to sing the songs of his people and dream of the life he was willing to curse the entire Isle to have once more. But as he laid down, he sobbed so violently that he began to shake. Magic pooled, a mist appearing around him most mystically and mysteriously. And in that moment, the king knew his time had been bartered. The deal he had tried to strike too powerful, for it was clear now that death could not be bartered with. Death could not be stopped once it took hold.

He had saved his daughter—his Orlaith—and he knew in his heart that if he could only save one thing, he was glad it was this.

As the mist began to cloud around the king and his deceased queen, he closed his eyes and two tears ran down his cheeks. Laying his head down, forehead touching hers, he only wished he had a moment more to say goodbye to his daughter. He knew it to be true, as the wolven king had said when he tried to barter all that he could ever have.

Their daughter would reign, and she would retrieve all they had stolen from them.

As so, it was prophesied.

And he was at peace.

~

The Prophecies of the Maesters
A Manuscript
Recovered from Volume III
Date Unknown

There once was a prince who was set to rule by birthright.
There once was a prince who was destined to wield the swords of
both men and women.
There once was a prince who was on course to have all power
concentrated at the tips of his fingers.

There once was a prince whose eyes danced with challenge and fought off the joys that he earned.
There once was a prince whose soul craved another, someone stronger than both him and his counterpart alive.
There once was a prince who was drawn to things he could not have and should not want.
There once was a prince who struggled with the depths of despair.
There once was a prince who did not smile nearly enough.
There was a prince.

And there was also a queen.
There once was a queen who was ruled by a desire for what was taken from her lineage.
There once was a queen who tried hard not to smile.
There once was a queen who deflected her joy and tried to turn it into anguish.
There once was a queen who dreamt of nothing.
There once was a queen who wielded her father's sword.
There once was a queen who was everything the world did not know they needed.
There was a queen.
And may the light guide her toward her crown.

PART I
COMHRAIC

CHAPTER 1

ORLAITH

Present Day

Orlaith, First of Her Name, Queen of the Elven Kingdom of Criostal, and the Rightful Bearer of the Emerald Crown kept a straight face as she walked through the crystalized Hall of the Deceased. Her head did not swivel, nor did her eyes stray from the step in front of her. Emeralds, sapphires, rubies, and diamonds alike coated the floors of the castle and shimmered like a thousand untold stories.

Though, if one looked at the Queen, she was merely bemused by the gifts from the Gods Just and Mercy.

Crowned on her sixth day of life, Orlaith was used to the enveloping beauty of the castle. If anything was less than, she seemed to shine less in comparison. The jewels, like most things these days, were merely how things were.

"My Queen," a voice whispered behind her.

She did not have to turn her head to deduce they were slowing their steps, the fear of slipping on the cut jeweled floor the greatest nightmare of some of these men.

Orlaith silently wished she could share her nightmares with those who served her.

Maybe then her kingdom would not have so many problems.

Without turning to face the voice that so unprofessionally addressed her, she whispered back. "May I help you, Alby?"

"Orla—my Queen—I require your assistance in the library."

She stopped, her heels colliding with the jewels in a heart-stopping finality. "And with what, might I ask?"

"There is urgent information."

Irritation nearly erupted from her light, yet she kept firm. A hall of crystals was a dangerous place for a wielder like herself to be, especially so caught off guard. She had no desire to blind anyone innocent.

Today.

"And about what, might I ask?"

Alby audibly gulped behind her. "About the *crown*, your Majesty."

Without another word, Orlaith had turned and exited the Hall of the Deceased.

ORLAITH WALKED CALMLY behind her servant, Alby, despite the thundering of her heart. She was incapable of hiding the sweat that pooled on the nape of her neck, her discomfort clear at the mention of the crown. It had been nineteen years since the crown had been in its rightful place, in the Kingdom of Criostal, yet it had felt like hundreds. Despite never laying eyes on the mythical object herself, Orlaith could feel the power of it thrumming lightly against her skin—like a soft breeze on a cool day.

The power was weakening and had been for years. And it had been the King of Teine who had stolen the crown, the ultimate display of power on the Isle of Ire.

He had taken it the day she was born, the day her kingdom was at its weakest. And for that, she could never forgive herself. Orlaith found comfort in the secrets her father had detailed in his journals all those years ago. The powers of the crown were not what they seemed.

It was a shame King Ahren had never tried to put it on, for she dreamt of him turning to ash.

Smirking at the sycophantic thought, Orlaith rounded the corner of the violet castle walls and blinked to rid herself of the painful memories of her birth and crowning. To be a child and know nothing but the raw power of one's position was more difficult and complex than she was willing to accept more often than not.

She had her dalliances—her ways to escape—but she could never shed herself of what it truly meant to be who she was.

It was maddening.

Silently, Orlaith continued to trail behind Alby toward the library. The only sound that pressed against the jeweled dark hallway was that of the queen's breath, unsteady at the mention of her point of vengeance.

The crystallized doors ahead glistened with the secrets of the library, and Orlaith found her lips curling up at the sides as she continued to fantasize about the Emerald Crown. She breathed through her power, pushing it down further and further until she was absolutely certain she was not going to take whoever it was that had stopped by to pay her a visit by surprise. Amethyst, emeralds, and obsidian danced on the doors as they welcomed her approach.

Stones always welcomed the Queen of Criostal.

Alby stopped as they reached the doors, their long brown hair billowing behind them. "My Queen, he's in there."

"He?" Orlaith asked before she had a chance to think. She cursed herself silently, despising when she spoke out of turn. Some part of her—a part she had tried to long lose—remained human, *common*.

Shaking her shoulders out and running an impatient hand through her white hair, Orlaith stepped forward without another glance at Alby.

The doors groaned with the weight of the crystal decorum as she stepped through the threshold. She was met with the scent of old leather and the stench of ink. The Scripters must have been writing—again—chronologically going through the events of the day she was born.

She would know, for she had commanded it months ago. There had to be some sort of explanation as to why her father had given up the crown so easily; some detailing of a trade must have taken place—

Her turquoise eyes searched for the visitor to whom Alby

had spoken. Rounding one of the three major bookcases in the middle, she nearly collapsed with the shock of the enemy in her home.

Dark hair tied behind his head in a tight knot, brown eyes as amber as the leather of the books before her, and the same familiar smirk of the portrait she had stared at since her twelfth birthday stood before her in all of his stolen glory.

"King Ahren, whatever do I owe the pleasure?" Orlaith nearly hissed, her elven instincts fighting to take over. She kept a hand placed on the hilt of the sword which was belted across her chest, not allowing Ahren to feel for even a moment that he was in control. Its name was Oidhe, and it was her best friend.

Well, besides Dealla.

But Oidhe did not talk back. Far more agreeable.

"You are much more beautiful than even your mother," Ahren said after a moment's pause.

Orlaith spat, rage consuming her like fire from within. "How dare you speak of her—"

He raised a hand impatiently. "Think what you'd like, Queen of Criostal, but I was not the one to bring about her death. We both know who is responsible for such a tragedy."

Without even a second to think, Orlaith was on him. Not even a breath of notice before her sword was placed upon his jugular, threatening to do the unthinkable.

Not missing a heartbeat, Ahren replied cooly, "I always figured you'd be more like your father. So full of *life* and *passion.*" There was a hint of humor mixed in with utter sarcasm, and Orlaith, in that moment, was not sure if she could have ever hated him more. She had seen him on more than one occasion in her life, but it had always been brief, and the Maesters had always taken care of it due to their regency together.

But now Orlaith was regent to nobody. The crown was not shared.

She owned it all.

"Tell me what you want, and what you're doing here, or I will end you."

He laughed, and for the first time, Orlaith realized his elven ears were decorated in emerald earrings from point to lobe. Smoke nearly came out of her ears in respite and disgust at him for coming to her castle and wearing a memoriam to what he had stolen from her.

"There's so much pain within you, my Queen. I fear for the state of the Isle if we continue like this." He gestured to the sword at his neck.

She lowered it, her breath coming fast.

"Elves live a long time," he continued. "Though we are not immortal."

"Get to the point, Ahren," she murmured in irritation.

"I propose a truce between our people. Men, women, children, and elves have lived in harmony in these lands for many years, thanks to your father. The Wars of Old brought us together after a fight nobody wanted. For nineteen years, your beloved regents have besieged our lands in respite for what we have—"

"For what you *stole*," Orlaith corrected.

"The crown was made for the true ruler of the Isle, Orlaith," he hissed, amber eyes flaring in rage. "And it is only right that it sits in my half of the continent. In my kingdom."

"Then why don't you wear it?" She smirked, knowing damn well why the King of Teine did no such thing. "I know Michael did."

"Because it is not mine to wear," he answered simply.

She wished he would admit the truth, and he would acknowledge his greatest weakness.

"At least we agree on something."

King Ahren barked a laugh, leaning casually up against the bookshelf behind him. Orlaith noticed for the first time the dark circles that sat under his eyes and pondered the longevity of the monster that stood before her.

Yes, elves were not immortal. Though often, they felt it. The thing nobody wanted to discuss.

Age.

Her people were not immortal, not without the power of the Emerald Crown on the Isle. Her father had not worn the object out of fear that he was not the one true king. For everyone in her line had passed down the same secret in one way or another. If one were not the *true* ruler —deemed by the two elven Gods of Just and Mercy—the crown would be placed atop one's head, and one would end in ruin if they were not deemed one of the Gods themselves.

Her father, by whatever means, had come to the conclusion that he was not blessed as his father had been before him.

Though not wearing the crown, yet owning it, had consequences. The immortality of her people demanded the crown be worn, and it had been cowardly of her father not to try. Even if her father had not been blessed by Just and Mercy, they would have accepted his sacrifice—his life would have been worth *something*.

The end of one monarch's life was worth the salvation of thousands of elves.

Teine had stolen the crown out of the belief that one of their monarchs was willing and able to wear it, to give life to their people and the Isle as many had done before. Yet, it had been fifty years since the crown sat atop an elven king or queen's head the way it was supposed to be worn, and the Isle was beginning to feel its absence.

Crop failures, continued battles, strong storms, and frigid winters were just the beginning of what would spiral into disaster if the crown was not placed atop a ruler's head.

And soon.

"I propose a marriage," Ahren said clearly, bringing Orlaith back to reality.

She nearly tipped back her head and laughed herself into hysterics, yet she kept a calm demeanor. He had already managed to rattle her, and she refused to succumb to it again. Instead, she replied calmly, an edge of war in her voice, "You would like to marry me? I am not sure that's legal, given our age gap—-"

"Just and Mercy, *no*. I'm afraid my time on the throne is coming to an end, my Queen."

Orlaith hid the shock that flashed within her. *He was about to abdicate?*

"I propose a ball of peace and an engagement to my grandson, Cathal."

She froze, considering.

He continued, "It has been too long since the crown has

sat atop a ruler's head, and your father and myself are to blame for the state of our world."

"Then why do you not put it atop your head if you want it so badly?" Her voice nearly cracked with frustration. It was not her father's fault. Not in the slightest.

"Because I know it is not meant for me." His voice was quiet, a change from the boisterous attitude when she had entered the library.

"Then who is it meant for?"

"When I was a boy, I received a prophecy from Mercy herself."

Orlaith quirked up a white eyebrow in response.

"She came to me in a dream and told me what must be done. I thought that it was to be my son who would wear the Emerald Crown—"

Prince Michael.

"And when he passed, after I ordered its taking, and tried to speak with your father, I knew I had made a grave mistake."

"Then why did you not return it?" Orlaith could not tell if he was genuine or not.

It was impossible to discern the lies from the truth at times, particularly when one grew up without anyone to do the discerning for you. When could he have tried to speak with her father? Before he passed?

"Because Mercy demanded that the crown remain in Teine until the Queen of Criostal was of marrying age."

Flames nearly burst from Orlaith's nose and mouth. He was not making any sense. She could not—would not—envision a scenario in which a God of the Elves had demanded that her kingdom was unworthy of the Emerald Crown.

"I will give you the crown if you marry my grandson."

Without another word, King Ahren strode past her and began to head toward the door. For a moment, he left Orlaith's line of vision. His navy cloak was the only thing visible as he sauntered toward the door. "I will await your response," he said behind him, not bothering to even turn his head.

After a moment's pause, Orlaith jogged after him. Her feet were soundless on the floor, yet she knew he could tell she was coming.

"Wait," she hissed.

He spun his head around, his face suddenly looking older than it had moments ago. "A response already?"

Orlaith knew the answer without even thinking it. If this was what she had to do—to stop the war and suffering—she knew she must. "I wed your grandson, and the crown is mine. Those are my terms." She needed him to bind it to her in words.

Elves did not make promises lightly.

An acceptance was a promise signed in blood.

Words meant something.

They always did.

"I accept it."

Orlaith smirked. She was sure she looked like Hell itself, a darkness radiating from her amidst the light of her power and physicality. "Then you may await *my* invitation."

CHAPTER 2

CATHAL

Cathal Ambrisona wandered the streets hooded, fearless, and utterly pissed.

Striding down the alleyways of Teine's capital city, Alexandriti, he kept a tight grip on the hilt of his dagger which was belted to his leathers. Although his elven nature blessed him with silence, power, and an unnaturally long life, it did not mean he was immune to the trials and tribulations of the rats of the citadel. Truly, he was on his way to the tavern, and he did not want to be interrupted.

With his grandfather—the king—away, Cathal dreamt of only one thing: ale and solitude.

As he rounded the final corner of the maze-like city, he found the place he was looking for. The Red Apple sat at the end of the dead-end alleyway, suspected as usual. *Perfect.* The most discrete tavern in the kingdom, the Apple never did him wrong. He was merely another body here, even could pass as normal. The loveliest place to forget how utterly un-normal he was.

For he was the elven prince of the Kingdom of Teine, and frankly, he liked to forget that piece of himself every once in a while.

Opening the grand wooden door with a thrust of his shoulder blade, he pushed past the numerous bodies of men, women, and elves as he made his way to the center of the tavern. The room was circular, oddly enough, and the place to acquire a pint of ale was located at the very center. Dark mahogany wood made the place feel as though one was suffocating, for it was so grand and crowded at all times that even the roundness could not make it welcoming.

The world had come a long way; men and elves living together in harmony under rulers who truly cared for the well-being of the crown, but they were still two rival kingdoms. And right now, the Kingdom of Teine had something that Criostal desperately wanted.

The Emerald Crown.

The piece of shit that had stolen his father from him, yet kept their lands alive. It was maddening, how fate and destiny intertwined in order to create life and death. He knew the teachings of the elven Gods would deem this to be the order of things, but Cathal was not ready to acknowledge that side of the world yet. Rather, he enjoyed the simple things. Solitude. Being alone. Daydreaming. Flirting without remorse. Dancing. Drinking.

There was so much to do when one simply did not give a fuck. And he was trying to enjoy more of this simple art, especially given the state of things as of late.

Shaking his shoulders and shaking off his impending memory, Cathal continued to push past the bodies of those enjoying themselves. "Excuse me, thank you, ma'am, excuse me—"

Making headway, he pushed past the final few bodies with the utmost politeness before he spoke with the rather large man who poured the alcohol. Acquiring his drink, he tossed a few coins at the man and walked away before he could look at him for too long. Before he had a chance to scout a place to stand—for there was no way he was about to sit—he felt a familiar hand perch itself atop his shoulder.

Turning, he met the ferociously blue gaze of Eowen with a smile.

"Cathal, what in the name of Just and Mercy are you doing here?" Eowen's tone was good-natured, but Cathal knew it was just so he did not draw a scene.

"Can I not go and enjoy the pleasures of life like a normal boy?"

Eowen rolled her eyes, running a hand through her long dark hair in exasperation. "Caw, you know you're anything but normal. Or are you truly that delusional?"

"You're not so normal yourself, E. This hair?" Cathal said as he took a deep swig of his ale. "This hair is too lovely to be normal."

"If I didn't see you come in, I would have guessed that you're already on the drink."

"And what brings you here? Stalking me again?"

"I was rather trying to escape myself," Eowen replied, suddenly looking far away. Eowen was the daughter of an elven general, one who served closely to the king. They had been friends for many moons, stuck at many counsel events together as youngsters.

And they had gotten into much trouble together.

Pinching between his nose, Cathal whispered in a near growl. "Just please tell me you did not invite Darragh."

Eowen barked a laugh, and anyone else would have nearly spit their ale if she was not so damn graceful. "I did not invite anyone. I came here alone, Caw. I had to get away from the council room, and frankly, away from my father. Things are bad all over the Isle. It is a little much to hear about all the time."

"That's what they always say," Cathal whispered as he took another drink.

He knew Eowen well enough to know she would understand his meaning, but also would not interject for clarification. That was the difficulty, one of the many, of being prince of the kingdom. He never knew if anyone was truly his friend. The power imbalance was great.

Without warning, a warm hand grazed the top of his black tunic, and he knew who it was without a second thought. Of course.

"Just and Mercy," Cathal whispered, pinching the bridge of his nose. He loved Darragh, for they were brothers of blood, but Darragh was not exactly the definition of solitude and a good time that Cathal had dreamt of on his walk down to this place.

Also, Darragh, by all accounts, was his only friend.

A permanent reminder that he had none.

None like Darragh, anyway.

"Are you not happy to see me, Caw?" Darragh asked, an auburn eyebrow raised in question.

Cathal knew he was playing with him in tone, but there it was again. The ugly rearing head of anxiousness that crept through Darragh like a serpent along the bottom of the sea. Nobody else would see it, or could see it, but Cathal.

The gift of brotherly love: bearing weights that the other does not even know they are holding up.

Cathal fake smiled, flashing the most dashingly sarcastic look he could muster. "You know I would never deny you, Dar."

Darragh snorted, his eyes nearly rolling into the back of his head.

Eowen chuckled to herself, clearly bemused by their banter. "Are the other members of your chaos brigade coming with you, Caw?"

"You know, if you keep calling me Caw, I am going to lose my reputation as the big bad Prince of Teine."

Now it was Darragh's turn to snort. "Who in their right minds thinks you are the big bad Prince of Teine?"

"Everyone," Cathal spat. "I am the grandchild of King Ahren, and our lands, if you have not noticed, Darragh, are quite bare at the moment. I am not exactly vying for ruler of the Isle's favorite monarch."

"Is there such a competition?" Eowen asked earnestly, her dark hair glistening in the candle light of the tavern.

"You're daft, Eowen." Darragh hissed.

"Brother," Cathal chimed in gently. "Play nice." Always on the defense.

Darragh's response was him drinking a sip of his ale.

Good enough for Cathal.

Darragh often interacted with spit-fire, but he had been rather stiff as of late. Cathal assumed it had something to do with the state of the Isle of Ire in general. The continent was in a state of disarray. Shortages of food had become a common theme, fires and earthquakes ran rampant, and humans and elves were starting to wage difficulties in fighting for these resources that were once everlasting.

As Prince of Teine, Cathal bore the weight of many of these trials and tribulations that his people went through. However, he also knew it was not all his doing. His grandfather, King Ahren, had a long and difficult history with the opposing Kingdom of Criostal.

And the Emerald Crown.

It had claimed his father. But that was a story for another day, one which Cathal would put off retelling and reliving for the rest of his life.

The Queen of Criostal, only the age of Cathal and Darragh themselves, was already legend. Unseen by many and kept away in her castle, Queen Orlaith was as much a mystery as she was a force. The Queen and King Ahren had long been at war, despite the Maesters running the show in her stead until her eighteenth birthday, which had been just last year.

"Isle to Cathal, I repeat, Isle to Cathal," Eowen said, waving her delicate hands in front of his face wildly. "Are you in there?"

"Yes, ma'am," he said, though he was still very far away.

It was ever-looming, this fight between the two king-doms, one which he did not completely understand. His grandfather was a giant, a legend among the elves, and had led all members of the kingdom of Teine to peace and prosperity.

But the Isle was clearly on a decline, and Cathal had no idea why.

"What were you thinking about?" Darragh asked, his voice melancholy, as always. Cathal knew, for Darragh's dark eyes gave away everything, even if everything else about him was utterly still.

It was one of his many weaknesses. Compassion.

Cathal had it too and sought to get rid of it on more than one occasion.

"I was thinking about Criostal."

Eowen stilled, and Darragh merely raised an eyebrow.

"Why?" Eowen said.

"Because there are two elven rulers on the continent, Eowen. And I'd love to know why they can't simply get along."

"We have two cultures, two leaders, two histories—"

"Two sides to every story," Darragh whispered.

If Cathal wanted to draw attention to such a dangerous comment, he would have hit Darragh right then and there.

Instead, he did nothing.

When it came to Darragh, Cathal would always do nothing. They were half-brothers, born from the same father. Prince Michael had taken Darragh in following the death of his mother, for both of them had died during childbirth, not uncommon for elves and elven children.

Despite their unique familial situation, it was not that unusual. Cathal's mother had been arranged in marriage to

Michael, as most royalty were required to participate in. Darragh's mother, to be blunt, was Michael's true love.

It did not hurt Cathal to think that Darragh was born of love, where he was born of duty. If anything, it made sense for him, and explained a lot of why he was the way he was. He was a necessity, someone who was not a creation of the Gods, but rather for them.

Darragh was the sunshine of the world, despite his rather grouchy and cloudy demeanor.

And Cathal was the clouds, despite all of the humor and sarcasm that burned within him.

And despite it all, they would do everything and anything for one another, for they were bonded by something deeper than brotherhood. They understood one another, and Cathal knew without a doubt that if given the chance, they would lay down their lives for one another.

Putting a hand on Darragh's shoulder, Cathal smiled softly. "Come, let us drink and forget things."

With a rolling of his eyes, Darragh smiled softly back, an acceptance to once again be whatever Cathal needed.

And so, Cathal drank until the sun came up, his brother at his side. As they meandered their way back to the castle, arm in arm, Cathal realized that Darragh had not touched his ale all evening, for he just listened. And he was whatever Cathal needed.

CHAPTER 3

ORLAITH

*A*lby braided Orlaith's hair in parts. The majority of her white locks were loose, flowing down her back beautifully in gorgeously divine waves.

Orlaith knew she was a queen, and she felt like it most of the time. However, there was always a part of her that hated the attention. The glory was rather unwanted in some moments, for it was difficult to have this eternal spotlight on oneself.

It was a lot to carry, especially if it was carried alone. Being the golden-haired princess—though it was more-so white as she had gotten older—proved to be more difficult than it was anything else.

Alby was kind. Alby was friendly. But Alby was not Orlaith's friend; she was very keenly aware of this. They would come in and braid Orlaith's hair. They would help Orlaith get dressed. They would tell Orlaith when the Maester of Borders was at the castle for Orlaith's swordsmanship training. They were a great asset to Orlaith's life, but they would never understand the fact that Orlaith carried certain things because they were weights she was born shackled to.

And she wanted to share this with them. For they were lovely and kind.

They were everything that Orlaith often felt like she was not.

Looking at herself in the mirror when Alby was finished, Orlaith admired their handiwork. Her hair was regal, while still encompassing all that Orlaith was on a daily basis.

Admiring her dark purple plain gown, Orlaith envisioned an Emerald Crown atop her head and smiled.

"Thank you, Alby. I appreciate you endlessly."

"And I you," Alby said in reply.

With a soft smile, Orlaith departed from her chambers and headed toward the endlessly darkened hallways. Lifting her fingers, she snapped as Alby trailed behind her, and the candles began to light as she passed.

She was to make her way to the courtyard, speaking of friends, in order to meet with her most trusted and most unlike herself. And she would need to see the way in order to make it to her.

Dealla Ravayarus.

As they walked in the overcast courtyard together, Orlaith envied the way the sunshine covered by clouds still seemed to hit Dealla Ravayarus' golden hair and dark skin.

Everything about Dealla was easy. She laughed and the birds would chirp. She would touch flowers, and they would seamlessly grow, as if trying to reach her hands as she passed by.

If somebody knew nothing about Orlaith, and they were told to guess which among the two of them was actually the golden princess, Orlaith was positive they would guess Dealla.

Orlaith had the opposite effect on the world—yes, her light could be radiant, but it was also dangerous. When she was four, the Maesters told her that she blinded a man who sang her happy birthday. When she turned ten and broke her arm playing in the courtyard, the world had shone so brightly that it took three days for the sun to shine again in Criostal.

The light that burned within her was too bright, so much so that it may as well be darkness. She shined too brightly, it seemed.

Dealla Ravayarus never understood that side of Orlaith, the one that could hurt almost easier than she could love. Yet, she stood by her side at all times, her fearless protector and closest ally in a world where chaos reigned free. Orlaith may have had the power of the light, but it was Dealla who captured its beauty.

"A ball?" Dealla was saying, her voice like wind chimes as they walked through the Criostal gardens.

Tulips bloomed endlessly this time of year, despite the cold and rainy nature of the Isle's curse. It defied all sciences, yet the maesters used to say it was the magic of the crystals which decorated the garden that kept the flowers alive, despite the violent weather the northern half of the continent experienced.

"An informal search for a husband," Orlaith hissed, tucking a white strand of hair that had fallen loose behind her pointed ear. "It's ridiculous, I know."

"I do wish you would tell me who your betrothed is," Dealla whispered low enough for just Orlaith to hear her. "You know I can keep a secret."

Orlaith chuckled. "You know you can do no such thing."

Dealla laughed, plucking a yellow tulip as they did another lap around the garden and tucking it behind her own ear. Lacing her arm through Orlaith's, she leaned in close to whisper once again. She checked behind her to make sure that Alby, who always followed them when they went on their strolls, could not overhear.

"The ball is *tomorrow*. What do you say we have a little fun?" Mischief danced in her eyes.

Orlaith nearly rolled her eyes, but for some reason felt like instigating this nonsense forward. "And where shall we have fun? Shall I invite the men and women of court to my chambers to watch us drink champagne?"

Dealla looked behind her to make sure nobody was watching before she shoved Orlaith playfully. Being that Orlaith was a high elf and a Queen, it would have been a major sign of disrespect for Dealla as a lower member of society to touch her sovereign as such. Yet, Orlaith and Dealla were not ones for the rules, so there was no harm in the matter.

And nobody saw. That piece was critical to all things in Orlaith's decision-making.

"You did that one time, and I still have nightmares about it, Orlaith."

"It was awful, but that's what made it such fun. To see the members of court just watch us drink champagne . . ."

"What if we went to drink champagne?"

"Not in my chambers?"

Orlaith was not sure she was following and was beginning to think she did not like the idea blossoming in Dealla's mischievous head. She averted her eyes to the other parts of the courtyard, suddenly thankful there were no guards around to witness this conversation. Alby was a kind soul and a blessed member of their royal household, but she was unsure what they would do if they had a secret larger than Orlaith being under the weather.

Which did not happen often, due to her elven nature, but alas, the point stood.

"I think we should go to Haversin."

Orlaith stopped so abruptly that the jewels on the hem of her gown rattled. Unable to hide her surprise, her hand flew to her mouth at the suggestion. "Are you mad?"

"Orlaith, if you are to be married to whomever it is that you refuse to tell me, you deserve to experience the world. I've been to Haversin. It's a few hours ride from the castle, and it's perfectly safe."

"Safe?" Orlaith choked out the word in a half-laugh and half-huff. "Dealla Ravayarus, I believe you have lost your mind. I will pray to the Gods Just and Mercy for your sickness to resolve itself."

"Orlaith, I am not sick, and you cannot tell me you have never dreamed of leaving the confines of your own castle."

Orlaith could not argue that it had never crossed her mind because it had. Over and over. For the last eighteen years of her life. "I cannot go. It is irresponsible."

"You have never been irresponsible a day in your life."

"And you have never had sense a day in your life. I am the Queen of—"

"I know you are the queen!" Dealla yelled, rain beginning to drizzle as she did so.

"Then you will stop this conversation at once."

Orlaith could feel the light beginning to build within her chest—clearly a sign that whatever her and Dealla were speaking of needed to cease to exist. The thoughts were dangerous, and leaving the castle was not an option. It never had been for Orlaith. She had duties. She had her legacy. She had purpose. Did Dealla not understand that?

They often had this type of argument. Her and Dealla. Dealla was freedom embodied, and Orlaith was duty embodied. They clashed like oil and water.

She turned to head back toward the castle, signaling to Alby to head inside and meet her at her chamber's entrance. Alby nodded, their shoulder-length brown hair curling slightly from the rain that had started.

A hand touched her elbow as soon as she turned away from her servant to find Dealla's blue eyes pleading. "You carry the weight of the world and the vengeance of your forefathers on your shoulders. Let me bear the weight of it for a night. Let me show you that the world is good and full of *fun* —let us end the duties of your life, put a stop to the burdens you carry. Come to Haversin, and let us experience all that your kingdom has to offer."

Orlaith huffed out a breath, and the word escaped her before she had a chance to register what she had said. But it was the expression of Dealla's face which signaled to her that she had said yes, those blue eyes exploding in excitement and pride at Orlaith finally choosing herself—for one night.

"If we ride now, nobody will miss us."

CHAPTER 4

DARRAGH

"Gods, Cathal, are you trying to take my arm off?" Darragh laughed, lifting his sword in revenge. Darragh dodged his brother's sword with all of the agility that lived within his elven bones.

Iron collided with the sheer will to dominate as the brothers of Teine contended for control, and Darragh pondered what it would be like to die at the hand of a sword. The clanging in the courtyard had drawn quite the audience. Women of court and nobles of Ahren's court remained onlookers, silently cheering and gawking at the display of adolescence which willingly played out before them.

On any other day, Darragh would have discouraged engaging with Cathal in this way—but today was not any other day. Today, Teine was expected to receive a long-awaited invitation to travel to the Kingdom of Criostal. It was a peace offering and a long overdue one.

Cathal had been awaiting such a letter since they had

returned home from the tavern a few nights prior. He had been preparing for his first venture to Criostal for the last nineteen years of his life, merely two weeks longer than Darragh had been.

Except, Darragh was a bastard, and his brother was the true heir to the throne of Teine.

But that was a fine detail, at least, according to Cathal.

With another *clang* and a step to the left, Darragh nearly dodged one of Cathal's advances with his longsword.

At the same moment, Cathal raised his blade, blocking Darragh's advances entirely. Darragh cursed under his breath, swearing he had just heard the women of court *coo* over the crown prince's advancements in their little battle.

Raising a dark eyebrow, Cathal smiled one of his impossibly sarcastic grins, and nodded his head to the side casually. It was an invitation to press on or give in. And it was one that Darragh had been all too familiar with for the last nineteen years of his life. "Do you yield, Dar?"

Darragh nearly growled with irritation. It was one thing to be bested in the courtyard by your brother, but another to be bested by the crown prince. Ducking with a gust of wind on his side, Darragh dashed underneath Cathal's sword and shoved the entirety of his body weight into his middle. They toppled backward, breathless and laughing hysterically as they struggled to continue their battle.

Managing to rise while Cathal lay on the ground half-groaning and half-laughing—Darragh peered over him—his longsword, Rinn, lovingly poking at his chest.

"Alright, Dar, alright," Cathal said, brown eyes flashing

with hilarity. They could be children when they were not duty-bound. It was difficult to remember that at times.

Turning around quickly while sheathing his sword, Darragh greeted the men and women who looked into the courtyard. "Thank you for observing Prince Cathal's training session, ladies and gentlemen of Ahren's court. We will—"

Interrupting him with a shoulder-check, Cathal stepped forward, commanding the room as always without as much as a second thought. "We will be here again tomorrow. Please, if you would like, bring your own longswords and join in on the fun."

The crowd erupted in flattery, as it always did in the presence of Cathal. Stepping backward, Darragh took his rightful place four paces behind him. This was his reality, his due diligence. It was the payment to be made for being born out of love and passion, to be scorned while your counterpart— your better half—basked in the glory of all that life had to give.

His mother had been an ordinary elf, one his father had fallen into romantic patterns with. She had no presence at the courts like some of the elven bastards' mothers did for lords. Kings and princes had another set of rules.

Shaking off the momentary jealousy, Darragh breathed in and out. He held his breath on the exhale, prolonging the release of emotions which these days seemed to linger longer. There was no animosity among him and Cathal, rather if anything, he did not envy his brother's position in life. But lately, there was a sense of strife between them; though it was unsaid, it was ever-present. It was difficult being the brother who had less.

Cathal's booming laugh snapped him out of his trance, only to be nothing less than unsurprised that his charming brother had found himself devoid of all sense and involved in a conversation with the notorious Aoife Tavish.

Darragh's eyes nearly rolled out of his head.

Adorning a velvet red gown, Aoife's bland brown hair shone as dully as it would in the shade, despite her being in direct sunlight. Yes, she was beautiful, but so were all of the Elves in the two kingdoms. Darragh nearly scoffed, for he had never been to the Kingdom of Criostal, and therefore, that would not be an accurate judgement. But the women of Teine were so beautiful that he imagined Criostal was no different.

Not that he would admit that to his brother or grandfather.

Or anyone.

Ever.

There was something about her that was so completely and utterly awful. Distasteful. It was not personal, but rather something he knew he felt within himself. His father, Prince Michael, had told him on more than one occasion as a boy of love. And what it really meant.

Darragh had been present for similar conversations with Cathal and Prince Michael, though the conversation often turned to lust versus a true soul connection.

Darragh had always wondered if that was why Prince Michael had fallen in love with his mother, even for that one moment when he had been conceived. It made it easier that way, coping and breathing through the bouts of shattering.

And that was what happened to Darragh when he

thought about his mother too deeply. It was shattering. Completely and utterly shattering.

And Darragh, for all his imperfections, had a nearly perfect memory. It was one of the many gifts he had that he kept to himself.

He remembered everything.

"Why do you entertain such vile company?" Darragh whispered to none other than himself.

"What was that, my darling brother?" Cathal asked, his amber eyes dancing. Clearly, Darragh was not as simple as he had thought prior.

"Nothing," Darragh said, just loud enough to demonstrate his discomfort toward the situation. Cathal had many skills in life—wooing young women, practicing with a sword, and sweet talking—but if there was one thing he was truly good at, it was reading other's emotions.

Sometimes he was too good.

Swinging an arm around Darragh's shoulders, Cathal stepped away from the lackluster Aoife and turned seamlessly with his brother back into the archway of the castle.

"Why do you insist on speaking with Aoife? Truly, Cathal, is there nobody in the castle who is not so bland and gossipy that catches your eye?"

"Darragh, if I did not know you better, I would say you were judging your crown prince."

Darragh snorted, resisting the urge to smack Cathal upside the head. "Not at all, brother. I am merely concerned about your marriage prospects. You do turn twenty in a few months."

"Please refrain from continually reminding me," Cathal grumbled.

Together, they pressed on through the castle's entryway. Teine's ash colored stone and dark candelabra's familiar eerie glow seemed to soothe both of them with its calming ambiance the further they walked into its threshold. The Kingdom of Ash, for all of its faults, was their home. Darragh operated under the understanding that nothing was perfect, and the sooner you started to embrace that truth—well, the sooner you could really love all that stood before you.

Their swords clamored behind them, dragging and sparking against the stones ever so slightly.

"Pick up your sword, brother," Darragh commented in irritation, realizing the blades were to be ruined if they continued. "We will have to have the maesters sharpen these again."

"Then let them," Cathal laughed, his arms stretched wide at his sides. "We are the Elven princes of Teine, after all."

Darragh blew a red strand of hair out his eyes, noting that he more than likely needed a cut in the next few days. "Correction, brother, you are the heir to the throne. Or have you forgotten I am a bastard?"

Cathal's dark features went taut, his eyes clouded in shadowy amber flecks. Putting his right hand underneath his brother's chin, he lifted Darragh's gaze until it was in line with his own. "But you are *my* bastard. Do not let anyone forget it."

"You are impossible."

"And you are impossibly dreary, brother. Come, let us indulge in the joys of courtly life." He extended a hand dramatically as he jumped backward and soundlessly landed in the steps ascending to the ballroom.

"I think I have indulged plenty for the moment," Darragh sneered.

Quicker than the wind, Cathal moved to stand in front of him. "What's got your tongue?"

"Nothing," he whispered, attempting to shove past him.

As always, the heir stood in his way, begrudging and selfish, despite being so in tune with what others needed.

"I want to go up to my chambers, Caw," Darragh sneered, his teeth flashing.

Retreating, Cathal lifted his hands in resignation. "Very well, brother, very well."

Darragh did not look behind him as he silently padded up the stairs and shut the door to his bedroom with a thud.

CHAPTER 5

CATHAL

Cathal found boredom in most images of his life. If he were to break it down: his childhood, his relationship with his brother, his complicated feelings toward his grandfather . . . It could all be brought down to moments. To images.

An image of him being crowned the prince at his father's funeral.

An image of him cradling Darragh as a youngling through the pain and suffering of losing his mother and the aftermath of grieving eternally.

An image of him flirting, of dancing, and of getting drunk in villages to simply avoid the task of being.

An image of fighting. Something he loved to do.

The heir to the ashen throne—and the crown of Teine— yet he found himself positively bored with his humble courtly life. By the time of his twelfth year, he had spoken to every noble girl and almost every princess on the Isle. He had danced in every ballroom but one and swung every sword that needed two hands to grasp it.

Snapshots. Images. They would capture it all. It was not much to surmise, his existence a necessity.

Cathal had lived and danced and played the part of prince well. The Kingdom of Teine had recognized him as the formal heir upon the death of his father—on his first birthday.

Prince Michael had been beloved by all, especially Cathal. His mother had died in childbirth, something which was common for most elven royals on the Isle. The birth of an elven child was something left for the maesters of health to be mastered, something as unpredictable as the storms of the seas themselves.

But King Ahren had demanded that the Emerald Crown be placed on the head of his only child, and Teine had suffered greatly for it.

Cathal had suffered greatly for it. The memory of his father dissipating into ash with a single breath . . . He pushed it away, deep below into the cavern of his soul.

Despite the respite, Cathal did not blame his grandfather for the death of his father. Michael had demanded, upon the recounts of others, that he at least try to wear the emerald crown. Facing rejection was just one part of life, especially as a monarch of the elven people. The crown had taken his father that day, but it had not been completely lost, for his spirit had been absorbed by the Gods Just and Mercy. His father's death had not been worthless.

There was purpose in giving to the Gods.

There was purpose in *trying*.

Cathal sat on an ordinary navy and gold chair in the hall of his grandfather's castle. The dark walls crept with shadows, and the scent of ash was thick in the air. Black candelabras burned scents of cinnamon and red wine, almost so lavish that it was nauseating. He breathed it all in, slumping against the back of his newly claimed and randomized throne in a display of utter boredom. Draping his hands on the arms of the chair, he tapped with his black painted fingernails the thrum of one of his favorite courtly tunes.

Impatience ran thick in the air this day. It was no wonder Darragh had dashed up the stairs in irritation at his mere presence.

Cathal wished sometimes that he could just *be*, instead of being who he was in his natural state. He knew he was proud, boisterous, and matter-of-factly too much for any one person to handle. His position only inflated his sense of self, his ego merely a sneeze away from being completely out of control.

Footsteps sounded down the hallway, and Cathal's whole demeanor changed. He sat up, his eyes now alert instead of sleepy—lost in thought. His grandfather had warned him that this letter may come from Criostal, an invitation for the century.

When he had asked him why such an invitation would arrive from the enemy, his grandfather had merely shrugged, though Cathal knew that such a gesture indicated this was anything but a casual moment.

As a leader of the elven Isle, Cathal knew he was expected to marry, eventually. There were many noble girls, many lords who would give their daughters up for a chance to have heirs to the emerald crown. But Cathal was not bound to these laws and tribulations of his ancestral ways. The people of Teine would expect this of him, but something always rubbed him the wrong way about an arranged marriage. He was not sure what type of proposal would come from Criostal, for he had never dealt with the rivaling kingdom, but he could not imagine it would be any type of offer of peace.

His kingdom had stolen the crown, only because Criostal had been too weak to grasp its power for themselves.

Scoffing to himself, he cleared his throat. He knew he was acting brutish, rather than diplomatic, but the misfortune of the whole continent stemmed from the inadequacy of the Criostal history. The people of the kingdom had harbored the crown, practically begging for someone to grasp its power. The Gods Just and Mercy were angry, and this strife was their punishment.

As the steps slowed to a halt, Cathal met the eyes of his half-brother. Darragh's gaze was filled with a wistful nature that had not been there when they had departed a short time ago.

"Brother?" Cathal asked softly, trying not to seem too eager.

Darragh bowed his head slightly in greeting and reception. It took everything within Cathal not to roll his eyes at the formalities of his princely position. Darragh did not deserve to bow to anyone. "From the Kingdom of Criostal, it would seem."

Cathal stood without a sound, his elven tendencies inhumane, despite the pounding that thundered within his chest. "What could they want?"

"Only one way to find out, brother," Darragh chided. "It looks like some sort of invitation."

"Grandfather said as such," Cathal replied, thinking back on his grandfather's cryptic sentencing earlier.

With still hands that felt as though they were trembling, Cathal used a pocket-knife to cut open the turquoise seal and top of the letter. Immediately, he was struck with the scent of tulips, nearly causing an asthmatic attack.

"Dear Gods," he choked out. "I hope the whole kingdom does not smell like that!"

Darragh snorted, taking the letter from his brother's hands while he was mildly incapacitated. "Let me do you a service, brother, and read it for you."

Cathal walked over to the chair he had claimed as his momentary throne before and sat down. Darragh paced back and forth as he read the letter, the scar on his face seemingly disappearing and reappearing with each turn. Cathal did not take his eyes off him for a second. The anticipation of finding out what in the name of the Gods the Kingdom of Criostal wanted nearly had him losing a grip on all of his elven qualities. Poise, weightlessness, and stillness were all on the verge from evaporating off his person. Images. Like paintings. They would have captured it all.

For some reason, he did not think he would mind shedding the qualities that made him as such. The magic, silence, and the speed, however, he would miss eternally.

Darragh paused, his amber eyes wide and his mouth slightly parted in surprise. He touched the tip of his left elven ear softly, a nervous tick that Cathal had come to realize over the years.

"You are touching your ear, so it must be good," Cathal said, all humor drained of his voice.

"It is an invitation to the castle."

"For what? A war meeting? A truce?"

"A party," Darragh said, a dark eyebrow raised in question of his own statement.

"A what?" Cathal could not hide the surprise in his voice.

"In a few days' time, the Queen of Criostal invites those willing to travel to the Kingdom from Teine to a ball."

"And what is the purpose of this ball?" Cathal was nearly blazing.

"It does not say, but it seems entirely peaceful."

"Has anyone ever seen her before?" Cathal's voice was unusually bitter. Darragh only tilted his head to the side as though he was unsure whether to extend an invitation to whatever Cathal was thinking. "For all I know, the Queen of Criostal could be hideous. Whatever are we to wear?"

Darragh barked out a laugh. "I am sure the Queen of Criostal is not hideous."

"Have you heard otherwise?"

"I have not heard much about her, Cathal, though her kingdom is flourishing in comparison to ours."

"I heard she rules with an iron fist, she is no fun whatsoever, and therefore only assumed she is ugly because not many have seen her."

With an eye-roll and concession for the sake of time, Darragh chided in on Cathal's diversions from whatever he was *really* feeling. "You may be right, Cathal, for she may be ugly."

Handing the letter over to him, Cathal read silently.

The writing was gorgeous and personalized. He could tell this was no mere servant, nor the magic of someone else inking it in her stead. No, this was a cordial invite to him and all of his kingdom's constituents. It was a power move.

Darragh sometimes played chess. Although Cathal had the intelligence but not the wit for it, Darragh destroyed him in it every single time. It was because Darragh was calculated. He lived his life like that.

This power move from the Queen of Criostal? It was calculated.

He wondered if she played chess.

If she did, she was probably legendary at it.

Maybe she would play with him when he met her at the ball.

With one last look at the repellent scented invitation, Cathal spun on his heel and moved toward the staircase without another word. Crinkling it in his hands, he tossed it behind him. It was dramatic, but to his case, he would remember what it said.

"Where are you going, brother?" Darragh's voice carried behind him up the stairs. He was rather shocked that Cathal did not want to take it further, as he always did when it came to their dynamic. In normal circumstances, Cathal would make some inappropriate comment, Darragh would ignore said comment, and then Cathal would eventually pester Darragh so much that he too would concede and make a twice inappropriate joke.

Cathal, it would seem to the wandering eye, was a bad influence. Though Darragh only knew him as a fierce protector and the Isles' best brother.

Without turning around, Cathal yelled back to his brother, "To pack, of course. I cannot wear my worst clothes if I am going to meet the ugliest queen."

CATHAL HAD BEEN SUMMONED to the throne room as soon as the sun had set.

Strutting down the darkened hallways of the castle, Cathal tried to remain calm. His grandfather had raised him and raised him well, but he was nonetheless the King.

And the King was not to be trifled with.

Black wax dripped down the candles which lit his way, his feet silently padding against the dark stones as he rounded the final corner toward the throne which would one day be his.

He strode through the entryway, for the Kingdom of Teine did not bother with any ornate doorways into the domain of the King. He paused out of respect as he spotted his grandfather straddling his throne casually, his dark hair pulled back as it always was. Except there was a scowl on his face, and that was what perturbed Cathal so.

"Your Majesty?"

"Come forth, Cathal."

Soundlessly, he walked toward the throne, his head bowed in respect.

Ahren cleared his throat. "I have a task for you, boy, one which I do not take lightly."

"Whatever you may need, I am here to serve," Cathal replied out of both instinct and fear.

"Our Kingdom is dying, Cathal, this we have known for sometime."

Cathal kept his eyes down, yet could not hide the slight tremble at the words which he knew to be sure. And they had been for some time. Teine was not full of grace and glory as it once had been, rather it often amounted to ash, and its elven people were wasting away.

The words lingered heavily in the air as Cathal fought not to spit them at his grandfather. *Because you killed Michael. This is why.*

Ahren continued, "I may ask something of you, Cathal, when we get to Criostal, and when the time is right, I am going to need you to comply. You may not question me, and you may not run from your duty to this kingdom."

Cathal nodded, his eyes still glued to the floor.

"Look at me, Cathal."

His head snapped up to find the king mere feet away from him. His amber gaze was filled with a dark intensity that would have frightened Cathal as a boy, but now just reminded him that the crown was lonely and cold. It was a reminder to Cathal that he was unworthy and not ready to resume such responsibility.

He much preferred courtly games to kingship.

Maybe he should take up chess.

"You are dismissed," King Ahren said, turning before Cathal could get another word in. "You are not privy to know yet, but know your allegiance is critical to our success. To our goals."

And just as soundlessly as Cathal entered, he left, afraid that if he were to linger, the King would put yet something else on his shoulders.

CHAPTER 6

CATHAL

They had been riding for hours. But when they arrived, Cathal could do nothing but gape at what stood before them. The legends, in part, had been true.

The Kingdom of Criostal was mesmerizing.

The brigade the Kingdom of Teine had brought with them arrived in Haversin as the sun began to set in the sky. The citadel's walls were—against Cathal's lack of will to admit such a thing—beautiful. Crystals lined the tops of the golden gate, gleaming when the sun hit them with a light that was unlike anything Cathal had ever experienced before. He thought that if he looked too long, there was a chance he would go blind. He did not know what the stones were: deep purples and dark greens with gray detailing . . .

Whatever they were, Cathal knew not to pry. He felt their energy, the gate nearly thrumming with it. So, the Kingdom of Criostal was powerful after all.

The elven men behind him thought they were whispering, though Cathal's sense of hearing was better than most, and he caught every word. They attributed the ambiance of the gates to the Queen of Criostal, who apparently possessed a light that could bring darkness to the world as much as it could illuminate.

Cathal had heard similar things over the years—that the Queen of Criostal had gifts beyond being born onto the throne.

But so did he.

He smirked.

It took a lot within Cathal not to turn around and humiliate them for speaking in awe about the monarch of the other kingdom, when their prince rode a horse not but fifteen feet away. He relented, however, and instead rolled his eyes at the gossip and speculation. He was no stranger to such spotlight and found it rather unimpressive in general.

Darragh, as always, seemed to read his mind on the matter. "Unimpressed with the rumors of the queen? I thought you two were to play chess?"

Cathal clicked his tongue against the roof of his mouth in a manner of both disrespect to Darragh and command to his horse Firefly. Her dapple hair under the disappearing sun shone like ash, and he felt comforted by all that she was. They had been paired for the past ten years together, bonded in friendship and journey as most elves in Teine were. They picked up the pace as they trotted along the cobblestones, approaching the inn that Cathal's brigade would be sleeping at.

King Ahren would be traveling to a castle on the border of Criostal and Teine and would be making the journey in one day. They had deliberated amongst one another for days on how they would amount both the prince and the king to Criostal for the ball and had decided upon them traveling separately. If either of them were to remain inconspicuous, it would be Cathal.

After tying up their horses outside and ensuring with the young elves that worked there that they would be given hay and fresh water, Cathal bid farewell for the evening to Firefly and made his way toward the inn.

Appropriately named the Haversin Inn, the ambiance was far more homely than Cathal would have originally expected, given the entrance and the state of the gate. Light wood decorated the floors and walls, the tables in the entrance packed with humans and elves alike, even some who Cathal could tell were half-elves. The welcoming environment seemed at odds with what Cathal would have anticipated from the kingdom which had been battling at their doorstep, though he acknowledged those in the tavern were just a small piece of the kingdom at large.

They strode in together silently, their feet soundlessly moving across what he assumed would otherwise have groaned under the weight of ten normal men. They walked silently, moving in uniform, toward the large table at the back of the building. Sitting down without as much as a whisper of the wind, they ordered a pitcher of red wine and potato leek soup. As it was brought to them, Cathal noted the homely smells of vegetables and the clear care that was put into preparing the meal.

Thanking the two men who had brought over their orderings, the five elves present dug into their feast of soup and wine, enjoying one another's company as though they were in their own kingdom. Still, the weight of the invitation held heavy in Cathal's pocket, ominous and a constant cloud in the back of his mind.

Belanor, a young noble elf from the citadel of Alexandriti, spoke to the elves about his speculations of the ball. Cathal could tell that Darragh and the others were listening, frequently chiming in with their own ambitions and prophetical idealisms about the ball. Their ideas ranged from a trap to a feast, simple or complex. Though none of them felt like the truth to Cathal, who sat with his hand on his chin as he sipped his wine steadily.

"Are you OK?" Darragh's voice cut through Cathal's mind like a sword through air.

Startled, Cathal shook his head. "Just thinking, that's all."

"Do not hurt yourself," Darragh whispered, shoving Cathal lightly on the shoulder.

After flashing him a look worse than death itself, Cathal laughed and turned to look around the tavern. Despite his elven qualities, the ride had left him bone-weary. He may have an extended lifespan compared to that of men, but he was not immune to all human characteristics.

"We can head up soon, your majesty," Belanor whispered softly.

"I am fine," Cathal said a little too quickly, despite his eagerness to retire for the evening.

There was something completely and utterly captivating about watching those who dally around this place—this city.

There was a sense of carelessness that he had never seen before in the city of Alexandriti, or even at his own castle.

And he was so fucking happy that the place did not reek like that blasted invitation did.

Turning around again to watch those who strode in and out of the front door, Cathal found himself met with the most unusual looking girl. White hair tumbled down her back in chaotic waves, almost as if she had been riding through rain. Her skin was so fair that Cathal would believe she had never seen the sun until today, her cheeks lightly flushed on her high cheekbones as though the wind itself had placed the pink there. He was not used to seeing females dress in anything but gowns, a privilege within itself. But something was off about this girl, for the clothes seemed to look unnatural on her.

As if she was meant for more.

As she turned, he tried to avert his gaze, but her eyes caught his immediately. Sea glass eyes darted through him, unveiling him to the point where he was nearly blushing in his chair. He turned his head quickly, trying to recover from the second long interaction to avoid—

"Cathal?" Eowen's voice shot through him, bringing him back to reality. He could nearly feel the laugh budding on her tongue. "Cathal, do you know her from somewhere?"

"No idea what you're talking about, Eowen."

Darragh snorted beside him, though nobody but Cathal would be able to tell that he had gone deadly still. "What was that?"

"No idea what you are talking about, brother," Cathal

chided again, though it was less convincing when spoken to Darragh as it had been Eowen. "Shall I get another pitcher?"

Cathal stood without waiting for a response, though he was sure it would be a resounding yes. Making his way toward the front of the tavern where the wine would be refilled, he focused in on his hearing.

A voice like sunshine flooded in as he angled his thoughts toward the sea glass girl, though he could tell it was not her voice that he sought out.

"Do you know that elf from somewhere?"

The girl grunted in reply, and Cathal found himself smiling at her resilience. So, her friend had noticed too that they had nearly been locked in a trance with one another.

Interesting.

Cathal walked up to the front of the tavern and lifted the empty glass jug of wine to signal that he required more. He laid down a few golden coins as the woman at the bar refilled it, her gaze nearly burning into Cathal's at the large sum he was paying. He flashed a charming grin before he turned and walked away.

And ran right into the sea glass girl.

"You might be the worst elf I have ever seen," she growled as she floated to the side of Cathal. "I am not sure I have ever met a klutz before who was not human."

The wind was nearly knocked out of Cathal, his power completely eroded as he took in the voice that had just —*insulted him.* Blinking twice, he opened his mouth to reply. She lifted a dainty hand, her long fingers held up as if to silence him.

"I will accept your apology. Have a great evening."

The golden-haired girl beside her snickered, her blue eyes nearly wet with an emotion that Cathal could not care to place.

They turned around and headed from where Cathal had come when he finally found the word he was looking for. "What?"

The sea glass girl turned around, her turquoise eyes dancing with challenge. A strand of white matted hair fell in front of her eyes, and she tucked it behind a very pointed ear. Anxiety rose within him that this was an elven girl, for he could not afford to cause a scene before he was admitted to the palace of Criostal.

"Do you not speak the elven tongue?" Her question was genuine, though her eyes were anything but a sea glass colored inferno. If that combination made sense.

"I do."

Part of her upper lip raised in a snarl. "Then why can you not say more than two words at a time, klutz?"

"I am not a klutz!" Was he shouting? Blinking, he realized he was. What the—

"That is four words, and I am unconvinced."

Before he could stop himself, the challenge from the petite elf resounded in his royal blood. He could hear his brigade and Darragh standing from the table, though to anyone else they would move soundlessly. Clearly, they were going to intervene in whatever this was.

Chuckling, he lifted his arms in exasperation. She was half his height. She looked like she was hand-crafted by the Gods themselves, yet the way she spoke . . .

Shock reverberated within him. This might have been the first woman who did not fall at his feet.

He took a step forward, towering over the white-haired beauty as he hissed, "You might want to watch your tongue. You do not know who you are dealing with."

A challenge. A promise.

Instead of backing down, she leaned forward. She smelled of rain and diamonds—the only scent which Cathal could place oddly enough. Her whole aura was something beyond what she looked like. Puzzling. Madness. He hated this more and more by the second.

"And you do not know who *you* are speaking to."

"Brother." Darragh's hand landed on his shoulder, tugging him toward the stairs.

Cathal continued to clutch the wine, as if holding it was a win within itself, as he was dragged up the stairs and to his chambers for the evening. It was something about Darragh's voice, however, that brought Cathal back . . .

The door slammed behind them as the elves funneled into the large room meant to house all of them. As soon as the door was secure, Darragh spun and was face-to-face with his brother.

"Are you an idiot?"

Fon smirked behind him, their black hair glistening as the fire behind him crackled. "Caw, you are the least inconspicuous elf on the Isle."

"Rattled by a dainty little elf girl," Belanor chided, shaking his head from side to side.

"What got into you? From the moment she walked in, it was like we had lost you." Darragh's voice was laced with fury, his hands clenched so tightly that his knuckles were turning white.

"I do not know," Cathal's voice was merely a whisper.

Darragh stood, impatience bristling off him. "I am not sure if you are aware, Caw, but if we were to be discovered traveling with the crown prince of the Kingdom of Teine, the few of us that stand in this room have sworn we will lay out our lives to get you to safety."

"I am well aware," Cathal groaned in reply, still holding the wine.

"Are you? Because you were pretty reckless for someone who claimed to honor such a feat."

"I am sorry, OK?" Cathal yelled at nobody in particular. "She got under my skin, that is all. It will not happen again."

"You are right. It will not because we are staying in this room until the sun comes up, and we make our way to the ball."

Cathal snorted, but it was Eowen's expression that had him wishing he could take it back.

"Sorry, Caw," Eowen said sadly. "Your safety is everything."

"I have to agree, Caw," Folen muttered sadly, speaking for the first time since they arrived at the tavern. Cathal knew he had royally messed up if Folen was contributing to the conversation. "We do not know anything about that girl. What if she is a spy? What if she works for Criostal?"

"What if she is ordinary? Just maddeningly so," Cathal jested, though he did not believe it himself. There was nothing ordinary about the challenge in her eyes, the way she pushed when he pulled . . .

"You and I both know you do not believe that," Darragh offered, running a slightly shaking hand through his hair.

Opening his mouth for a moment to inquire what had Darragh all up in a tizzy, Cathal decided it was against his better judgement. He was sure it was nothing.

Though he could not shake the nagging feeling that his interaction earlier with the white elf was nothing but extraordinary.

And annoying.

Setting down the wine jug, his chalice of victory, Cathal crawled onto the velvet plush chair in the corner. Wrapping a woven blanket around himself, he leaned his head back and tried to wash away the memory of the elven girl's sea glass eyes.

CHAPTER 7

ORLAITH

Unbelievable.

Nearly shaking with irritation, Orlaith looked toward the door where *he* had just been escorted by his comrades. Insufferable.

Men. All of them were idiots.

Especially elves.

"Dealla, you promised me that I was to have fun this evening, and all I have gotten is almost in a fight with an elven idiot."

"Orlaith, I had nothing to do with that." Orlaith was not looking at Dealla, but could practically feel her eyes rolling out of her head.

"You have everything to do with me being here."

"But look at your face; you're *smiling*."

Orlaith purposefully tried to frown, but found herself laughing instead. Dealla was right; the joy that was plastered across her face was one she would remember until the end of time. She would not admit it to anyone, but she hoped and prayed her face would hurt tomorrow, so this feeling and normalcy would last a little longer.

By the end of the day tomorrow, she would be engaged officially to the prince of the kingdom of Teine, but the crown would be hers.

And the crown was all that mattered. She had to remember that. But it was getting harder to separate this idea of who she should be from the feelings that just overcame her. In some part, maybe leaving the castle was a mistake.

It would be a destiny fulfilled, her dreams realized, and the end of the Isle's strife would be dealt with. She was the rightful heir—she knew it deep within her bones.

And she would wear the crown or die trying. That was that. There was no other way. No other option. She had simply run out of time, but that did not mean she could not enjoy this night.

Without warning, Dealla's hand grabbed her elbow as she tried to drag her toward the crowd of people who had begun dancing. Half-elves, elves, men, and women shoved the tables that had crowded the tavern room before to the sides to create a makeshift dance floor. It was hardly the balls of speculation Orlaith had attended prior, but there was a simplistic and wholesome nature to it that had her heart thundering in her chest.

Dealla flashed her a grin worthy of the Gods of Just and Mercy themselves, and they began to spin with the masses. Orlaith threw her head back and laughed so hard she swore she could have been roaring. Her white hair flowed freely behind her, unbound and knotted. There was an uplifting sense that there were no rules here, not ones that mattered to high elven society.

Orlaith was not constricted. Not confined.

She could breathe.

They danced to countless songs, intertwined with endless spins and twirls. Arms linked, they embraced the world for what it had to offer.

She embraced what it meant to just be Orlaith.

Dealla Ravayarus stood before her, looking quite immaculate herself in a blue opaque gown with yellow tulips all over the bodice.

In a whisper that was barely more than a breath, she hissed, "If the people of this bar knew who stood before them, well, they would be utterly entranced."

"Shhh," Orlaith replied, glancing around, suddenly afraid of being discovered, though to her surprise nobody was looking.

"Come," Dealla said, grabbing her arm. "Let us powder our noses before we return to the festivities."

"What in the name of Just and Mercy do you mean by powder my nose?"

"I heard some lords' wives speaking in the passageways," Dealla said, her eyes dancing like they always did when she was up to something. "And I believe I figured out the meaning."

"Are you going to tell me what it is, or are you going to leave your queen waiting?" Orlaith hissed between her teeth.

Dealla leaned close, her dark skin shining with the pomades and glitters she had been decorated with this evening. She truly was a marvel. "It means to become more beautiful, if that's even more possible for you, your Majesty."

Despite her efforts to constantly remain neutral this evening, Orlaith blushed at the compliment. Sweaty and exhausted, Orlaith leaned close enough to Dealla's ear that she would not be overheard.

"I am going to take a breath outside."

Dealla paused, obviously concerned about letting her queen out of her sight. "Are you sure?"

Orlaith lifted the black men's tunic she wore at the waist, showing off the dagger she had strapped there before they left the castle. "I will be fine."

Dealla grabbed her by the cheeks, apprehension blatant on her face. She wore all emotions on her sleeve. "Come right back."

Nodding in reply, Orlaith strode out of the tavern. The relief was immediate, the sweat that had begun to feel like a part of her suddenly freezing against the sputtering rain and dropping temperature. She closed her eyes as she took another two steps away from the open tavern door, the drizzling sky as cleansing as it was refreshing.

Turning to admire the tavern, she gasped at the sight of one of the elves who had pulled away the idiot from earlier.

He had dark red hair, cropped close to his head, whereas the idiot had been messy. Amber eyes shone almost like midnight, unforgiving and impatient. Yet what was most striking about him was the long, jagged scar that ran from the bottom left of his nose to the right side of his jawline.

Whatever—whoever—had done that to him obviously meant to hurt him.

"Can I help you?" she asked pompously, baiting the unknown elf for no good reason she could think of. She was ready for round two of whatever had happened earlier, especially since this elf looked like a more formidable opponent.

He snorted, lifting his arm to show the dagger that sat at his waistband. His leather pants moved soundlessly in the night, his heavy boots not even trotting against the cobblestones below.

Ah, so he was a high elf as well. Interesting.

"Come to get some fresh air?" she asked, though fear was an undeniable tremor in her voice.

Cursing herself slightly, she was unsure why she was breaking down. A moment ago, she was fearless, and now when faced with him, she found that something within her was squashed. Ferocity was gone, and all that remained was uncertainty. Could she take him?

Backing up, her back quickly hit the building behind her. Bricks rubbed against her spine unevenly, her breath quickening. Was this what it was to panic?

Lifting his dagger, he dragged it carefully across her jawline, positioned so perfectly that she was forced to look him in the eyes. "What makes you think you can speak to my brother that way?"

Her voice sounded from her before she could even blink. It was hard as steel, iron as her own dagger, which was strapped under her dark tunic. It was the voice of a queen who had been crowned on her sixth day of life. Impenetrable and as divine as the Gods themselves.

"What makes you think your brother can speak to *me* that way?"

He grimaced, and the wind behind them picked up instantaneously.

"Apologize."

She nearly barked a laugh, cold and righteously evil in tone. "I will never apologize for the stupidity of others." She took a step forward, letting his dagger push into her jugular ever-so-lightly. "Now back away before I have your head."

The wind began to roar, and the scarred elf looked around as if to look for the culprit of the wind. After a moment's hesitation, he paused, and his gaze returned to Orlaith's. She recognized the look in his eyes all too well— fear. And it clicked for her then; he was doing it. He was the gust of wind. A high-elf indeed, confirmed before her very eyes. Except what she saw within him was something she recognized all the same in herself: a lack of control. The most terrifying emotion of all when it came to power.

She had never met an elf before that had a gift even remotely similar to her own. Though her gift was different in nature, he was also powerful.

Slowly, he backed up, his hands raised in submission.

As if in reply to whatever force was at work between them, her light surged ever so slightly. Although it was no more than a flash of lightning, it was enough.

"Shit!" she shouted, closing her own eyes in the hope that he did the same.

It would seem they had both lost control. A grip on reality. What in the name of Just and Mercy was going on?

When she opened her eyes, the scarred elf was left stunned, grappling for words and losing control of all that he had held together a moment before. The wind exploded behind them, glass shattering from the windows of the tavern and hay flying through the air from the stables. Another gut reaction, she noticed.

Well, this was going splendidly.

Orlaith fell to the ground, desperate for something to hold on to as the world continued to implode around her. She was momentarily depleted, her strength leaving her as he overtook her. She looked up amongst the chaos at the boy, who was utterly horrified at what he had done. He had reacted to her reaction, as she had to his. Recognition flashed in his eyes as he saw her after her light, and she saw him mouth a phrase she had known all of her life, yet never referred to herself by.

"The light of Orlaith."

Feeling utterly and completely daring, she smirked. For the first time in her life, she greeted the phrase not as an embarrassment, but as a form of power. "That's me."

"*No no no no no no no no no no no no no no no* . . ." He was barely audible over the wind, yet the word repeated in her mind.

Beginning to crawl forward, she pushed past him and realized for the first time that he was still standing, unaffected by the blasts of the elements behind him. Head down, she crawled forward again. The door to the tavern shut with the force of nature.

Grabbing onto the door handle, she stood and turned around. As she mustered whatever wind was left in her lungs and whatever command she had left within her after such an eventful evening of forgetting what her purpose was, it stopped. Her breath came back to her, her hair once again flat against the nape of her neck. She breathed in and out slowly, attempting to demonstrate poise, despite the reality that quickly hit her in the face.

He knew who she was.

Her light had revealed her.

In one heartbeat, they were on one another again, their hot breath on the other's cheek, and their daggers at the base of one another's hearts.

"If you kill me, it is treason," she whispered, challenging him, despite the terror that pulsated through her.

It was the most complex mix of emotions she had ever experienced, this infernal rage that had not left her earlier, but subjugated with all the fear her heart could muster. And her power seemed to recognize this, as did his, lashing out like a child who did not get what it wanted.

"I cannot let you go now that I know who you are."

She paused, pondering. "And who might you be? You have no right! This is my kingdom." Thinking fast before he could answer, she added, "Where is your loyal idiot? Clearly, he means a lot to you . . ."

"You will not touch him," he hissed.

"Then you will let me go, and I will not have your heads when I return to the castle. Like I said, this kingdom is mine, and anything you do to me can be considered treason."

He looked bewildered, clearly thinking of something he had no intention of telling her.

She smirked. Sweat dripped down the side of her face due to the tension that built within her strained muscles. She loved training and the show it put on, but as queen, she had been limited these last few months in preparation for her nineteenth birthday and official coronation ceremony. It was strenuous, pretending not to be exhausted when all she wanted to do was give in to the shaking of her muscles.

While she struggled physically, it was clear the scarred elf was terrified. Of what? She could not place it.

"This is the best offer you are going to get," she growled.

Without a second to spare, he backed away, both of them immediately sagging upon departing from one another. As she opened her mouth to reiterate that he and his idiot friend were not welcome in her kingdom, the door to the tavern burst open.

Dealla threw her arms around Orlaith, nearly sobbing with relief. "The door—it would not open!" She was scripting over and over, nearly inconsolable. "The wind was howling, the windows in the tavern cracking, and all we could do was stand inside and wait for it to be over!"

"It is okay. I am here," Orlaith whispered.

"I thought I lost you, your majesty."

Her voice was so quiet that she was sure no half-elf, elf, or human could hear her. She could, however, feel the weight of the eyes behind her coming out of the tavern to see what the ruckus was. As she lifted her gaze and turned her head back to where the scarred elf had been standing, she found herself dumbstruck.

The scarred elf was gone, as was the memory of the wind on her back.

CHAPTER 8

CATHAL

Cathal could have sworn that he woke up not in his own body. It was as if he was looking down at himself, detached as if he was completely and utterly losing his mind. What in the name of the Gods had he drunk last night? He did not remember it being a lot . . .

But when he opened his eyes fully, after a few more seconds of being completely and utterly lost, he woke to none other than Darragh in the room, who looked like death reincarnate.

"What happened to you last night?" Cathal asked, all charm and humor.

"I do not have time for your nonsense today," Darragh spat.

Cathal noticed a moment too late the dark circles that were visible under his eyes, and the fact that he had not changed out of his dark tunic and leathers from the night prior.

"Are you alright, Darragh?" Concern flooded his voice.

It was not unlike Darragh to wake up in a mood, but never would he give Cathal the cold shoulder. Was he mad at him from the night before when he almost got into it with the sea glass girl?

As always when it came to Darragh, Cathal found himself rapidly spiraling. "I am sorry, brother. I did not know the white-haired elf would challenge me like that. I did not have any intention of speaking to her. It was completely unacceptable for a crown prince of the Isle to act as such—"

Darragh cut him off with a raised hand and shot him a haunted gaze. "We should not speak of the white-haired elf on the rest of our journey."

"Noted," Cathal chided, sitting up in the chair he had fallen asleep in. He rubbed his eyes, the morning falling off him with each passing second he was awake.

Slowly, Darragh stood. He wavered slightly in his step as he did so, as if he were bone weary. Holding his tongue, Cathal rose as well. He made a mental note to ask Darragh about it again later—it being whatever was bothering him—and try to raise some type of emotion other than negativity from him.

"We must be off," Darragh said starkly. Clearly, he did not want to partake in this conversation anymore, but Cathal knew it could not be avoided forever. "Grandfather is here."

"Here?" Cathal asked, his voice a little too quick to answer.

"That is what I said. Downstairs," Darragh replied, pointing with his index finger below them. "We are to travel the rest of the way together."

Cathal opened his mouth, but Darragh was already out the door.

Gods save him, he thought as he rose and followed his brother down the creaky tavern steps. Despite his elven nature, it was a testimony to how old this building truly was. The fact that it still made noise, despite his light-footed gifts, was rather impressive. The Kingdom of Criostal was nothing like he had anticipated, being that they were rivals at their core. Yes, that rivalry was by design, but it was also one that continued to fester. There had never been forgiveness on either side.

Maybe it was time someone stood between the kingdoms and pleaded for reconciliation.

As Darragh rounded the final turn of the wooden staircase, the bottom of the tavern floor opened up again. King Ahren stood at the threshold of the room below, which was now empty compared to how it had been last night. Cathal nodded to his friends as he approached his grandfather with a bow, slightly blushing at the memory of last night acting like a fool in front of the white elf.

Shoving off the memory of her sea glass-colored eyes, Cathal shook his head and rolled his shoulders as he dipped in greeting.

"Cathal, you may rise."

Cathal, as always in the presence of his grandfather, did as he was told. "Grandfather, Darragh tells me we are to travel together the rest of the way."

"Yes, we are to make the journey with one another, in a demonstration of strength against the Queen of Criostal."

"And why are we invited to such an event?" Cathal knew

he should not worry about the details of this match, but he could not shake the feeling that there was some hidden agenda behind this invitation.

His grandfather's words were haunting, especially being that they were the queen's guests.

"The Queen of Criostal and I have business."

Cathal did not need to turn to know that Darragh had an eyebrow raised.

"Are we privy to know what this business is?"

"In due time," King Ahren said softly.

"We are not walking into a trap, are we?"

King Ahren smiled softly, placing a long, bejeweled hand on Cathal's shoulder. Yet, it was Darragh behind him that he made eye contact with as he said, "There is no trap, yet I would still keep your wits about you. The queen is powerful, sharp, and full of wit. The Gods are on her side in more ways than I would care to admit, and we would be fools to expect this evening to go off without a hitch."

With his free hand, he beckoned one of his guards behind him to bring forth a chest. "The queen has requested that the ball be masked to enhance the peace between our two kingdoms. It will dull the ways in which we can see our differences and blind us to what we would see if there was nothing to hide behind."

He reached into the chest and plucked out a white bejeweled mask which would tie around the head with a white satin ribbon. The mask had two slits for eyes and would cover one's eyebrows and partially unveil their under eyes.

Handing it to Cathal, he said, "I picked this one out specifically for you, Cathal. Make sure you wear it well."

Cathal ran a thumb over the delicate beading in the design of numerous snowflakes and raindrops. "It is beautiful, Grandfather, my King, thank you."

Ahren smiled, flashing his devastatingly white teeth. "Come, Darragh."

Darragh stepped forward soundlessly against the old wooden floors, and Cathal found himself wincing slightly at the remembrance of how catastrophic he must have sounded walking down the stairs a moment ago.

"For you, Darragh, I have selected an ash gray, a symbol of our kingdom and all that we have endured."

Cathal noted the stillness of his brother as a slightly trembling hand received the honorable gift. Darragh touched the top of his ear slightly with his free hand, his other grazing the topaz jewels that flattered the ash-colored satin and fabric.

"I do not deserve such a beautiful mask, Grandfather—"

"Silence," King Ahren said sternly. He gestured to Cathal and continued, "Both of my blood deserve something beautiful for such an occasion. You are both cut from the same coin, though you could not be more independent of one another. I have never seen such a beautiful relationship between two brothers, and I have never been prouder of the young elves you have become."

Darragh wiped his left eye, and Cathal found himself putting a hand on his brother's shoulder in comfort instinctually.

"Grandfather—" Both started in unison.

King Ahren held up a hand to stop them both. "There is no need for words this day. Come, let us head to the castle. We have a ball to attend."

CHAPTER 9

ORLAITH

She had gotten back to the castle completely and utterly pissed. Not in the sense of drinking too much, but rather, the emotion. The evening had been nothing like Dealla had intended, and although it had definitely been an adventure, Orlaith was left incensed.

Clearly, she was not meant to be one who had fun. This would be the last time she tried.

Dealla had been nonsensical when Orlaith told her that upon their return. She pleaded with her queen not to give up just because of one circumstance, one moment. But Dealla clearly was forgetting who she was speaking to. And what was about to befall them all.

Looking in the mirror, Orlaith fought with her choice of an emerald gown. It was perfect in the sense that it would match perfectly when she wore the emerald crown later. She had the dress fitted to hug her petite frame closely, while holding her integrity as Queen of Criostal. The gown was strapless, straight across the bust, and dusted with golden flecks. It hugged from the top of her, through her waist, and flared out slightly at the bottom.

But it was just that, a momentous plea to the chains and shackles she wore. The ones that would ensure last night was her last chance to be free and whatever she wanted.

For a brief moment, she thought of the elves she had fought with the night prior and smiled.

The elven seamstresses deemed that the dress style was referred to as *mermaid*, for the women who swam on the northern border of her seas but did not come ashore. She loved honoring the women of the sea as such and requested that they be sent jewels as a thanks for the inspiration behind something so beautiful.

There were so many creatures of the continent that Orlaith did not know of personally, but only heard of them through stories. She had a memory of learning about wolven, centaurs, fairies . . . All the creatures that had left the sight of elves and men upon the downfall of her father.

It was all tied to the crown. The harmony of the world.

It was suffocating.

Recentering, she looked in the mirror once more. Her white hair was worn straight, a few strands that formally fell loose tied behind her head with an emerald ribbon. Golden bangles danced freely on her wrists, and emerald studs pierced her ears.

She looked like the queen she was always meant to be—divine, righteous, and full of emerald power.

Glancing at herself one final time in the mirror, she admired the work of her elven maids. They had done a spectacular job of pulling her together since she had been asleep so late in the day. The night prior had drained her, especially due to the fight that had transpired.

The memory of the elf with the scarred face haunted her since she had awoken, yet it also set something afire within her. Her life had been rather bleak, due to the trauma of her childhood and the courtly position she held in the world. But the battle with that boy had been something she had never experienced; it was real and raw. It was power. It was harsh. It was *fun*.

Despite her best effort, a part of her she could not ignore had awoken.

She was glad, for the sake of her kingdom and herself, that she would never have to see that elven boy again. Yet the memory of how they had fought would stay with her for the rest of her days.

It was an awakening of the light within her, and she refused to dull its brightness now.

Lifting the emerald mask she had picked out for herself, she tied it tightly around the back of her head. She had requested all guests that arrived at the castle wore a mask, so they may have an evening of peace amongst the kingdom. There would be no judgement, no rivalry. There would just be elves, men, women—individuals who would come together to celebrate the Isle's healing and the crown worn once again.

They were to be saved. All of them.

～

ORLAITH WAS NOT SOFT. She had been hardened to the world since the sixth day of her life: crowned without a family member to be regent and raised by the maesters of the Isle.

Yet, as she strolled through the familiar crystalized walls of her castle and noted those that walked around in harmony, she could not help but hold back tears. The diverse crowd of women, men, children, and elves was harmonious and breathtaking because it was so unusual. Never in any history that Orlaith had learned did she know of a moment quite like this one.

And it was because of *her*.

A humbling and awe-inspiring moment.

She nodded to those as she passed, though without her crown, and with the mask, she knew it would be near impossible for anyone to recognize her. There were some rumors of her appearance, beautiful and young. Yet nobody knew much about her, rather they knew her story.

Orlaith was an orphan, and her crown had been stolen from her. But it was the pain that her people and the people of the Kingdom of Teine suffered because nobody wore the crown that was the focus of the world.

It was rightfully so.

Suddenly, Dealla's voice sounded behind her. Although she was not so subtle, she would not reveal her identity by using her true name. "Or!" she hissed, grabbing her elbow.

"Yes?"

"I have heard rumblings that King Ahren is amongst the crowd."

Orlaith nearly laughed. "Of course he would be. I invited him."

"But you have not seen him yet."

"I am sure he will reveal himself in good time," Orlaith reassured her. As they approached the balcony off the ballroom, Orlaith gestured to Dealla. "I am going to get some air. I will be there if you need me or find any gossip worth sharing."

"Glad to see your night away from the castle did not change you, Or. Stubborn and all business, as always."

Orlaith almost opened her mouth to tell Dealla she could not be more wrong. Last night had changed her in more ways than she could reconcile. The memory of the scarred elf flashed through her mind, and she shut her eyes quickly to avoid continuously thinking of him and that blast of wind. They had to be connected somehow.

Without warning, Orlaith connected with something solid. She paused, lurching backward and holding up her hands in resignation. "I am so sorry for running into you. My apologies—"

"You? Capable of speaking without an ounce of sarcasm dripping off of your persona? I have to admit I am surprised to see you here, but I am more shocked to hear a lack of vehemence in your tone."

"*Klutz.*" Orlaith nearly fell over as she gazed up at the idiot elf from last night.

"Ah, there she is."

"What are you doing here?" she spat.

"I was invited."

She nearly hurled. Of course he was. Pausing for a

moment to collect herself and find a word to express what she was feeling, she landed on, "Charming."

He laughed, tipping his head back. The diamonds that danced in the light off his white mask were dazzling, as were the amber flecks in his dark eyes that glowed in the moonlight. "Good to see it was not just the drink of last night that created such a persona from you. It is good to be true to yourself always."

The sarcasm that dripped through his every word was nauseating. She nearly shoved him, but instead tied her hands behind her back. As she opened her mouth to reply something snarky about how he was an idiot, a voice cut through the air and straight through her heart.

"Caw, Grandfather has requested us."

She spun, her white hair twisting through the air as her eyes snapped up to look at him.

The scarred elf.

Despite the gray mask he wore, she could tell he immediately recognized her. He opened his mouth to respond, but clearly could not find the words as she struggled simultaneously to find her own. They were both fumbling, falling, and incapable of forming coherent sentences. And thoughts.

She had never felt so helpless and overwhelmed in the presence of an equal match.

And she silently prayed to her power to stay silent, as she was sure he was doing right now too.

"Do you two know one another?" Klutz whispered, awe laced in every vowel of his question.

"No," they both hissed at the same time.

"Interesting," the idiot huffed out, striding toward the scarred elf and leaving her in the dust.

"Where do you think you are going?" she asked, unable to let either of them out of her sight without an explanation of where they were going.

This was *her* house, after all. *Her* home.

"To meet with my grandfather, who was also invited."

She rolled her eyes, but despite her best efforts to calm herself could not. "But we were not finished."

The scarred elf stopped walking.

The idiot, unsurprisingly, continued. Turning his head slightly, his dark eyes met hers with a haunted expression. "We were."

And then he left her standing, incoherent and shocked.

Nobody spoke to the Queen of Criostal like that.

So, she followed him.

CHAPTER 10

ORLAITH

Orlaith was so irritated by the presence of the klutz that she followed him and nearly fell over when she realized whom his grandfather was.

"You have got to be joking—" she shouted, the room turning to look at her in shock. Before them, she was usually poised, calculated. Now, she had lost her wits.

And she was not sure when she was getting them back.

King Ahren stood at the forefront of Orlaith's kingdom's chamber council, and she nearly lost her mind at the sight. She was chomping at the bit, her ferocity barely hidden behind her permanent scowl and snarl at everything he said as he commanded the room like he mattered in Criostal. She wanted to scream at him that this was not Teine, but she knew she had to keep her feverish rage under control in front of her council. They barely trusted her as it was, being that she was so young, and she was, above all else, a female.

Cathal stood irritatingly still for a klutz against the wall, his rage clearly matching her own at his own disgust with this entire situation. She wanted to mouth to him that he was an idiot, and she was with him against this.

Whatever *this* was.

The Maesters that sat in front of her threatened to push Orlaith over the edge. She was maddeningly frustrated with not being the center of attention, but she justified it because she had been since her sixth day on this Isle.

Literature, Stars, Medicine, Horses, Farming, Borders, and Advising all sat straight up, their violet robes in matching unison. To make matters worse, despite their very presence, was that they were not saying anything. King Ahren stood before them as he spoke to them as if he were at a tea party, telling tales of how he had come to see the beautiful Queen of Teine, and how she had accepted him with open arms, as well as the proposal he had for her.

Orlaith's eyes nearly rolled out of her head at the whole thing, clearly remembering that when King Ahren had shown up in her library, she was not thrilled. She had agreed to marry the klutz for one reason and one reason alone.

The Emerald Crown.

Tuning in after cooling down her inner rage, she breathed in and out before opening her ears to listen to Ahren's spineless speech.

". . . Orlaith has been so kind to me since my arrival, a whole ball prepared just to join our kingdoms together before the big announcement."

The Maester of Stars lifted his hand to interrupt, his long blond hair so perfectly straight and his voice so proper that Orlaith nearly exploded on impact upon hearing it. "So, the two kingdoms are to become one? The stars were not aware of such a union."

"Well, it is not as if . . ." Cathal started, only to be silenced by the voice of the Maester of Literature.

His blue eyes shone with promise and excitement, though he was the only Maester who was now demonstrating any type of emotion.

Leave it to the elf utterly consumed by books to be the reality on this council of elder knowledge.

Then he paused, as if finally in recognition that Orlaith had not wandered in here as an elven woman with power.

She was the power.

And she was to be his betrothed.

And he was blindsided.

She almost felt bad, if she did not feel so bad for herself for being so blindsided by this. If she knew he was the Prince of Teine, she never would have agreed to this. There had to be another way to get the crown . . .

"Grandfather, you cannot be serious," he started, taking the words right out of her mouth. "You—" he said, turning to Orlaith. "You are the Queen of Criostal?"

"You can call me your Majesty, if it pleases you," she shot back, trying to put back on the mask.

She could have sworn she heard the scarred elf snort. She ignored that too, despite the twitching that was occurring on the sides of her lips.

"In the history of our two kingdoms, over the thousands of years, there has never been a marriage of this magnitude. It is positively splendid," King Ahren said with a soft smile.

If Orlaith was willingly participating in this in any way

other than to serve her own needs, she would have caught herself blushing at how genuine he was in his earnest response to the news.

The Maester of Borders, however, was not sharing in the thrill. "I cannot possibly see how this will function. The two kingdoms have responsibilities. They have different cultures. How are you expecting this union to work?"

Cathal looked at Orlaith, then looked at King Ahren. They were locked in a triangle of political discourse, and it was rather shocking that neither of them had an answer for that. Clearly, Ahren had an agenda that Orlaith was not aware of. And clearly, Cathal was catching on that he was not sure how he fit into all of this.

Orlaith breathed in and tried to do what she did best—bullshit. "Maester of Borders, I find that this is a peaceful evening, and I cannot foresee our cultures clashing."

The Maester of Borders snorted, his impropriety and rudeness triggering Orlaith's primal instincts.

She stepped forward. "Do you question the Queen of Criostal?"

"I guess I do, your majesty," he chided, his unkempt black hair glistening in the moonlight.

"How dare you!" she spat, her elven ears perking up as she knew she was beginning to flush red with rage. All sense of calm and kindness evaporated from her in an instant, and she could do nothing but fumble for the rage that blistered within her at this master.

He stood suddenly, towering over her. The display of toxic masculinity both shocked her and ignited her, and suddenly, the room flashed with the inner light that Orlaith no longer had a tap of control over.

Members of the Maesters screamed, and she heard the Maester of Horses scream to shield their eyes from her power. She rubbed her arms viciously, as if that did anything but comfort her.

After a moment passed, the blinding light ceased, and the room returned to normal, except for the shielded faces.

A pause, then King Ahren spoke, his voice filled with awe and wonder. "So, the Queen of Criostal does have a power."

Despite her best efforts to remain calm, Orlaith flushed. She was embarrassed, for she never lost a cap on her power in such a trivial way.

Before she could open her mouth to respond, the Maester of Advising stood, and he hissed in the old language, *"The White Queen will rise with the wind at her back. The Ash King will rise with the light guiding his way. The crown will be worn by the one who the Gods deem worthy, or the world will shatter. Ash and light will not be able to rein in the stars. The light will rise with the wind at her back. Ash will cloud the skies, for the souls of the two kingdoms will be matched in a duel for glory. The Emerald Crown will choose, and may the road rise to meet them when she does."*

The room was silent, and before she knew what was happening, everything went dark for the Queen of Criostal.

CHAPTER 11

ORLAITH

It always started slow.

And then everything fell away into blinding light.

It was consuming, like tripping and falling. At first, one thought they had control of the situation. There was a brief moment of, "I have this. I am not going to descend." And then it quickly transformed into panic, despair, and complete and utter fear. With the scarred elf outside the tavern, it had only been a glimpse of what type of power she beheld, but when it unleashed like this, well, there seemed to be no limit to what she would do. What she *could* do.

Fear. The thing that always dangled at the end of Orlaith's consciousness. The thing that she never wanted to acknowledge. There was no point in calling it an emotion, because it was something she did not want to simply *be*.

The heat was blinding and binding. Circumstances overtook her senses, and she could not even see an inch in front of her.

It was all light.

It was all bright.

It might as well have been darkness.

ORLAITH SAT up on the floor of an empty council chamber with a throbbing head and an idiot in her frame of vision.

"Are you alright?" Cathal's irritatingly smooth voice cut through the air. She had only met him twice, and yet the ring of his tone was something she would not soon forget.

"Quiet," she hissed out, extending her arm in a casual plea for him to help her up.

He accepted, grabbing and hoisting her to her feet with haste. It was as if he too did not want to touch her.

"I do not want to marry you, despite what you may think of my charming good looks and my dashingly princely mannerisms." She did not have to look at him to know he was smirking. "I do, however, quite wish that you would have told me who you were before we dashed into this council chamber. A heads up would have been spectacular."

"There is nothing dashingly princely about your mannerisms, you klutz," Orlaith replied with as much venom as she could muster. He was absolutely incorrigible, blatantly irritating . . .

"Ouch, your bark is worse than your light."

And disrespectful.

Orlaith moved to stand up and found that she was immediately dizzy. "I despise you."

"And I do not like you much, either, but my dearest grandfather has coerced you into agreeing to this marriage for the good of the continent."

Lifting her gaze lazily to lay her eyes on Cathal, she blew a loose string of white hair out of her face. "I agreed because I need something, and you are going to help me get it."

Cathal raised a dark eyebrow, his blueish green eyes dancing with interest and challenge. "What am I going to help you get?"

Orlaith smirked, relishing in the reaction she imagined she was going to get. "Oh, you know, it's gold, pointy, and is bedazzled in emeralds. Ever heard of it? Ever seen it?"

Cathal paled, and Orlaith barked a laugh. "You cannot be serious."

"You owe me one year of marriage, and then it is *mine.*"

"You can have it. I do not bloody want it."

Now it was Orlaith's turn to look surprised. "Whatever do you mean, you do not want it?"

"You heard me. I. Do. Not. Want. It."

"Then can I have it, and we skip the whole marriage part?"

Cathal snorted, rolling up the sleeves of his garb and exposing his forearms casually. She figured that most elves and women on the Isle would appreciate the sight of such a casual royal, but it rather infuriated her.

Why was he so much better than her, so much so that he could act so nonchalant and be deemed attractive for it? If she acted as such, nobody would take her seriously.

"I do not think my grandfather would allow such a thing. Clearly, he is getting something out of your agreement with him."

"You out of his life for the next three hundred and sixty-five days?"

"Very funny, Orlaith. Very funny." He shook his pointer finger at her in a mocking tone. "I think he said something of shared resources, reuniting the country . . . Or were you not listening when he spoke to the Maesters?"

"I hate the Maesters," she said without a pause.

That damn eyebrow raised again. "Do you like anything?"

"Myself."

"I rather doubt that." He raised a dark eyebrow in challenge.

Damn. He had her there.

"At least I can *balance*."

With a smirk on that gorgeous mouth of his, he replied, "Touché."

Putting her hands on her hips in defiance, she squared up to him. "You owe me this. At the least because your grandfather demands it, and he is your king."

Cathal sneered, those damned blue eyes dancing with irritation and a deep desire to challenge that she nearly admired.

Nearly.

"I guess you are to be my wife then."

"Do not sound too happy about it," she huffed in a laugh.

"I am thrilled, your majesty. Just absolutely thrilled."

Leaning down over her, he hovered with his gaze positioned challengingly at her own. "I always wanted a wife."

"Where is everyone else?" she questioned, realizing not for the first time that they were alone.

It was all-consuming with this elf, though she could not put her finger on why. It was not as if it were love, the type she had read about in books, where one would be blind to everything but one person.

Not at all. In fact, it was almost as if she was the villain in her own story, and he was her arch-nemesis. When she saw him, they were like magnets. Repelling. Yet they could not get enough of whatever drew them together.

He was madness.

And she was mad that she was anything but a queen when she was with him.

"I cleared the room," he said matter-of-factly. "My grandfather obliged, of course, thinking I should be the one to be here when you woke up."

She grunted in frustration, crossing her arms over her chest.

"So, the light thing, it is real?"

She nearly snarled, but made a conscious effort to keep her face devoid of all emotion. "You sound surprised."

"Believe it or not, Orlaith—if I may."

"That is my name," she replied dryly.

"Orlaith, you are a bit of an enigma. Did you know that?"

"Whatever do you mean?"

But of course, she knew what he meant. She was a secret. That light of hers was a fucking part of it.

"Why do you hide?" he asked, his princely mask dropping for a moment. "When you shine so bright . . ."

"It is not funny," she growled, flashing her teeth at him.

"I was not trying to be."

She heard it. The meaning. He was earnest.

That did not mean it was not annoying.

"I hide for the same reason everyone does," she whispered. "Sometimes . . ." She gestured around the whole room wildly. "It is all too much."

"Too much can be fun," he said softly.

"It can be too bright," she replied drearily.

He opened his mouth to reply, possibly ask another question, when she cut him off.

"I will see you later, Prince Cathal. Please tell your grandfather my status."

"Which would be . . .?"

Turning her head, she said, "That I am to be your wife." Her ears perked up at the sound of the lingering music, her elven hearing working overtime to reacquaint herself with her surroundings. Extending a hand, she waited for him to grasp hers.

"Are you not going to come with me, Cathal?"

With a smirk, he grabbed hold of her hand, and off they went to rejoin the party.

CHAPTER 12

Darkness blitzed beneath the embers of the ground that held up the Kingdom of Criostal. Howling winds swooshed and smacked against the vibrant trees that danced effortlessly through the aggression of the world's hand.

A black hand, covered in armor and soot, reached out to touch a petal which had been falling through the sky slowly. As the hand reached and reached, the petal free fell in what it anticipated to be an eternal dance. As pink made contact with black, the flower petal instantly wilted, and the tree wept as the wind grew louder and louder.

They had made it.

And the world was terrified.

CHAPTER 13

ORLAITH

Orlaith lived her life, until these past few days, in routine. She woke up, and every minute of her day had been planned to the nanosecond.

She expected what to eat, who was going to deliver it to her, who would piss her off, and how many beads of sweat would fall from her brow during training. She dreamt of nothing unusual, never remembering such thoughts at all because of their insignificance.

For Orlaith, life was predictable and revolving around one thing: the desire to regain the crown.

She redefined patience, confident that her time would one day come.

But for Dealla, her best friend, she was the complete opposite.

Dealla was alive with a ferocity of life and danger that Orlaith could not even conjure an experience of. She was determined to live life as though every second was anointed itself by Just and Mercy, a gift worth exploring.

Orlaith silently cursed herself that she was not more like Dealla, for maybe she would not have fallen under her coercion so quickly when the opportunity had presented itself.

They were the spitfire and the ember, and clearly Orlaith could not ignite without Dealla's flame.

Sitting up abruptly, and after an hour of pulling herself together, Orlaith made her way into the ballroom to find Dealla. As anticipated, it did not take long. Dealla was always one of the most boastful in the room.

She was sprawled out on a couch in the ballroom, the green velvet offsetting every gorgeous and rich feature that Dealla shared. Her gown was draped magnificently over her legs and bodice, and it was no wonder that a mirage of human men and women were gawking over her ethereal presence.

Orlaith cleared her voice, interrupting their—-whatever they were doing.

"My Queen!" Dealla shouted, standing silently and fast.

Orlaith simply raised her pointer finger and beckoned her to come with her. She needed to tell her everything that had happened—the light flaring, Cathal being the klutz, everything . . .

"So serious," Dealla chided behind her sarcastically as they walked down the crystalized halls to a safe meeting room. Neutral territory.

As the large white doors closed behind them, Orlaith spun. Her gown danced around her with motion, free and powerful.

Exactly the momentum she needed if she were to have this conversation with her best friend.

"There has been a development," Orlaith started quietly, pushing the confusing burst of nervousness that infiltrated her mind.

If she did not say anything now, knowing herself, she would never. Dealla would distract her, take her somewhere, and Orlaith could hide from whatever she had wanted to tell her. The ball was still raging on—it would for some time—and if Orlaith did not try to take control of the situation, it would take control of her.

But this could not wait.

"What type of development?" Dealla asked slowly, her eyebrows raised in confusion and perpetual humor.

"I am engaged to be married." It was one thing to tell a friend of a bad plan, but it was another to tell them of a stupid plan.

"Just and Mercy!" Dealla shouted. "Are you serious, Orlaith? To whom do I owe the congratulations? It has been confirmed?"

Orlaith swallowed. "Prince Cathal."

Dealla paused, the top of her lip twitching—and not with humor. "What do you mean, you are to marry the prince of Teine?"

"I need the crown, Dealla—"

Clearly, it was the wrong way to start with Dealla.

"But what about choice? You never had a fucking choice about anything in your life before, Orlaith, and the other night, you finally chose yourself. I was so proud of you and thought you were finally going to rise to meet the road you were always meant to walk."

Orlaith, for the moment, was speechless. "This is out of duty, out of sacrifice for the kingdoms—"

"Fuck duty!" Dealla shouted, her eyes blazing with irritation and bitterness. "You have never put yourself first, never. And now you have a chance as queen, in front of all of these people, to choose yourself."

"You do not understand what it is like. It is not easy being—"

"I never said it was!" Dealla said, moving toward her and grabbing Orlaith's fingers with gentleness. "But you cannot live this half life, Orlaith. You are not just an elven queen; you are an elf. And you deserve a life." She paused, her chest rising and falling in complete despair. "You do not know what the world has to offer. There are creatures beyond these walls, stories about the world just dreaming of being discovered . . . And you know none of it!"

"I am the queen—" she started, before Dealla cut in once again.

"You deserve love, Orlaith, real love. You deserve a chance to be happy and to breathe in the fresh air with someone who believes in you as much as you believe in yourself. You are too damn confident, too fucking powerful, to let yourself waste away in an arranged marriage in a grasp for power!"

Orlaith was speechless. Dealla was a lot of things, but she had never spoken to Orlaith like this before.

"Dealla, please. He can get me what I want." She paused, grasping her friend's hands as she whispered, "This marriage will get me what I want."

"Material, Orlaith. It is material. What about what sets your soul ablaze? What about what *you* need?"

"You do not understand," Orlaith said sadly, turning away from Dealla and toward the door. "Leave me, Dealla. I wish to be alone for a moment before I return to the ball."

Silence returned her request.

"Dealla," Orlaith said, command slowly entering her tone.

Her friend was allowed to speak her mind, surely, but she needed to respect that boundary which forevermore separated them.

"You may be my queen, but you are not my master." Dealla's arms were crossed over her chest in utter defiance. "You cannot do this to yourself, lose yourself. Orlaith, you mean too much to me—too much to the world . . ."

"Dealla." Orlaith's voice was straight venom, all patience gone and the queen returning her to persona.

She hated being like this. She hated being pushed to become what she oftentimes most hated about herself. These were the moments that haunted her dreams, losing everything again and again because of the crown that she wore. The role she was born into.

It was hard to not lose sight of that, though, when the crown was all she had. It had taken everything from her at one point, and she guessed it continued to do so, but she was too invested now. Too involved.

Being queen wasn't just her blood. It was her.

"The world is so much bigger than you even know. You do not know the scope of its reach because you're kept away with the Maesters! The world is so much more dazzling than crystals and princes—if you would only see that."

"You may be my friend, but I am your queen."

Despite these thoughts, the words regrettably shot out of her mouth.

She wanted to take it back. She wanted to apologize.

"Emeralds are not going to save us, Orlaith." She paused, her lips in a tight line. She was resigned. Orlaith had won. Then why did she feel so godsdamned awful?

"Is that all? Your Majesty."

And in this moment, Orlaith knew she had lost Dealla.

For certain.

For right now.

"Dealla! You will not walk away from me. I am your queen!" Orlaith's fists were balled at her side, her white hair wildly flowing in front of her face. This was how she was to react, like a godsdamned monster.

Like a monarch, instead of a friend.

Dealla turned, her golden locks trailing behind her in utter perfection as she looked at her best friend and said, "Is there anything else you need from me, your Majesty? Or can I go?"

"You are dismissed," Orlaith sneered in finality. "And do not bother coming back until you are willing to listen to what I have to say."

CHAPTER 14

ORLAITH

Orlaith and Dealla fought, but it never ended in
blatant defiance.

Until today.

But in Orlaith's confined life, she learned to cope with
her frustrations with force. So as soon as the door clicked
behind Dealla's angry voice, she was off to the training room.
Not bothering to change out of her regalia, she reached for
Oidhe in her chambers before heading off to the one place
where she could lose her cool without threatening to blind
anyone.

Oidhe was the word that defined her entire life. Her
father, her mother, her legacy, her Kingdom. It was the
bridge between her and all that she really knew of them, for
her time on the Isle with them was as broken as she was at
times. Though, she would never show it.

To show all the pain that lingered within her was to be
weak.

Orlaith was the Queen of Criostal, and diamonds were made under pressure.

Lifting the sword that was born out of the catacombs of her family's legacy, Orlaith relished in the gasp that erupted from the crowd before her. The Queen of the Isle had never been in public like this, and therefore all she did was a spectacle.

So, a show she would put on.

Standing at the precipice of her throne, the descent to the crowd below more demeaning than she would approve of if she were in control of the Maester's, Orlaith began her dance. The crowd whistled with praise as she twirled like a Warrior, her long white hair swooping behind her as if the wind itself was blowing it off her shoulders. Jaw set, she stabbed at the air and cut through it just like she had in all of her practices.

This evening, if she had not already, she would prove to the world that she was not just the queen that ruled behind the scenes with an iron fist.

She would prove to the world that she was that woman, and then some. And even though she did not know when that day would come, it would start with her awakening.

Something she could have sworn was happening right now.

Filling with courage, she began to run across her stage. Her gown flowed behind her in a blaze of glory, and with two hands on Oidhe, she jumped. Tucking her legs as she pushed off, she turned through the air and swore to herself that if she fell and landed on her sword, she deserved it.

With her breath held, she closed her eyes and gritted her

teeth against one another so fiercely it was a miracle they did not chip.

And she landed on her two feet with her sword raised in triumph.

Though she did not smile, she did not so much as blink, as she bowed to the crowd of the Isle's citizens and walked away from her throne and into the crowd.

Passing by those in front of her, silence fell as those realized they were now in proximity to the girl they had seen from afar. She greeted each that she passed with a resounding soft smile, not showing her teeth in case she did in fact break one in her display of perfection.

The music faded behind her, and she found it oddly fitting. She needed silence. She needed a break. She needed a minute to think.

"My Queen, you are a marvel," she heard a charmed voice say behind her, breaking her out of her consciousness.

She spun silently—a perk of her race—and gazed upon the brother of the elf she had figured she would see. The scarred elf.

"Ah," she said, trying to sound unimpressed, even though her heart thundered wildly in her chest. "You."

"You are just as bemused as I," he said rather dryly. "I did not mean to intrude."

"I came here for peace and quiet," she said. "It can be quite noisy . . . out there."

"I understand more than you know," he said, though that same curt nature still sat in his voice. "I saw your little performance up there. It was captivating."

"Be gone then. I am sure I will be seeing you around, pending my relationship with your brother."

Decidedly, she ignored his comment about her performance. She was not sure what she should be doing, but performing in front of the crowd felt most natural.

He chuckled, and in that moment, Orlaith would consider the sound dark, if that was an appropriate way to describe such things. "My brother is a lot of things. He is intelligent, quick-witted, dashing, and a fierce warrior."

He took a step closer, and Orlaith's breath caught in her throat unintentionally. "But he is also without ambition. He is kind, caring, and I would even argue it is to a fault."

"And why are you telling me this?" she growled.

"Because if you break him, you are going to have to deal with me." Silently, he took another step forward, though Orlaith noticed he was not as silent as she was, nor was he as loud as a human. "And I am not kind or caring, and I would not argue that it is to a fault."

"It was you at the tavern. With the wind." An admittance. Maybe even a damnation.

He stepped back, taken by her words as if he had forgotten the incident entirely. "It was you at the tavern. With the light," he whispered, a slight smile appearing on his facial features.

"Ah yes, a flaw of mind. Some would say I am too bright to a fault."

"It was magnificent," he whispered in a huff. "No fault present."

Despite all of the ferocity in her heart, she smiled. "Enjoy your evening, Prince Darragh."

"Wait," he chided, holding up a hand to stop her. "Darragh," he corrected. "Just Darragh."

"Do not dim yourself down so you cannot shine. I know a thing or two about that. I may have to for my own sanity and safety. But you? You may do as you wish. At least in Criostal," she drawled, stepping back with a courtesy bow. "As I said, enjoy your evening, Darragh."

He stood for a moment, and she debated whether he was sizing her up or deciding to continue before he took a deep breath. "And you enjoy your evening as well. I hope we can at least find peace in the idea of putting the continent on the same page. A united front."

She snorted. "United is one way of looking at things."

"That is why we are here, despite what you may think of my grandfather," Darragh said softly.

She could tell he was being earnest, despite his grouchy persona he projected.

"King Ahren is no friend of mine, but I will do anything I can to get what I want," she replied, looking down at her sword which rested between her two palms at her waist.

"Then we have something in common," Darragh whispered, taking a step backward toward the party. "I will do anything to get what I want too."

Without warning, she found a smile tugging at either side of her lips. "Good evening, Darragh."

"And to you too, Orlaith."

❧

AS HE DISAPPEARED through the passageway, she got back to wielding her sword.

Slashing the air for the next few hours allowed her to work through whatever it was, and all that it was, that was bogging her down.

She cut the air, and she thought of the marriage.

She thought of her father. What might he think of her in this moment? Was the crown worth all of this? He had chosen her over the crown before, but look where it had gotten them.

She thought of her mother. Was she in pain? Was she watching over Orlaith?

She thought of Cathal. What did he mean when he said he did not want the crown?

She thought about her fight with Dealla. Why could she not let it go between them? Why was she so defiant?

She thought about Darragh.

And refused to ask herself anymore questions.

So, she cut more at the air and did what she did best . . . pushed everything away.

CHAPTER 15

DARRAGH

Darragh could have cursed himself for being so reckless. What had he been doing? He asked himself, though he really knew the answer. What had he been getting at, finding the Queen of Criostal in the corridors of a castle that was not even his and engaging in a dangerous discourse?

He was wandering, trying to escape those demons that sometimes clouded within him. He was troubled, more than most. A perk his grandfather had told him of being the brother of a future king. There was this weight, this spectacle and realization of what the person who he loved most in this world carried. It sat on his chest and got heavier in situations like this. In places like this.

Courts like this.

He feared for his brother more than he cared to admit.

So much so that he had threatened a queen. If Grandfather found out what he had said—shit, if Cathal found out —he'd be something resembling dead meat.

His heart thundered in his chest as he wandered away from where he had accidentally stumbled upon the Queen of Criostal. He cursed himself again for simply standing there and watching her. For someone who he had observed did not get out a lot, she moved like she did. The air had been a formidable opponent; it always was. Like a mirror, training alone allowed one to focus and catch only flaws.

He knew the feeling, for he did the same thing sometimes when he could not sleep. He imagined something had been bothering the Queen of Criostal; for that was the only reason a monarch would leave their own ball to engage in a fight with the air.

Making his way into the outside courtyard, Darragh found himself in need of air. Badly. He needed to get it together, especially before another bout of panic took over him.

"What is that?" Darragh asked nobody in particular.

Soundlessly, he walked toward where the cracking of branches had come from. As an elf, his eyesight was superior to most, but the darkness was so deep that not even he could make out whatever had made such an indiscreet noise.

He had escaped the venue in order to clear his mind, especially running into the queen with her magnificent sword.

There were always storm clouds that loomed within him, but the storm clouds as of late had turned thunderously loud. To most people, they would seem damagingly loud and exhausting. But to Darragh, they were completely and utterly normal—if that was such a normal thing to be a part of.

Horror was the word he would use to describe what permanently lived inside his mind.

Due to the nature of his birth, an elven bastard to a continent famous king, Darragh often had to push aside the clouds that loomed over his head and life. He was always more broken than he wanted to let on. For there was true suffering and hatred that he always felt he needed to sift through.

But with Cathal, life was easier.

Cathal, being his half-brother, never looked at him with animosity or as a threat like other elven lords did. Even the Maesters seemed to loom over Darragh here, like he constantly carried a knife to be wielded over his brother. He was incensed by the idea that anyone would assume the worst of him when it came to Cathal.

For Cathal was the only sunshine in the world in which Darragh lived.

Even when Darragh had suffered his scar, Cathal never looked at him differently. It was a gift to be so accepting. One reason Darragh knew in his heart that Cathal was chosen by the Gods to play this role. This mediator between the two kingdoms.

"Hello?" Darragh asked again, for that storm cloud continued to brew over his mind. "Is anyone there?"

No answer.

He huffed a sigh, straightening up and smoothing out his black coat and pants before rising to readjust the mask he wore. As he did so, he felt the familiar brush of the long scar which ran across his face. Instead of admiring it as a symbol of his survival, he felt its weight tonight—something which he did not do often. He was completely and utterly out of fucking sorts.

Thinking of hitting himself, he instead rolled his shoulders forward, then backward.

"Get it together, Dar," he whispered to himself. "Get it together."

And then he made his way back to the castle and tried to silence the demons that existed within himself along the way.

CHAPTER 16

DARRAGH

Shaking off his weird experience in the courtyard, and still not entirely certain that nothing had been looming in the bushes, Darragh walked back to the castle to find himself interrupting a meeting between Cathal and the king.

There was a point in Darragh's life where he would not have dared to intervene in such a conversation, for fear of being improper. But Darragh quickly realized it was being improper that ensured the world carried on in the way it was supposed to.

So, he stepped through the doorway and jetted himself into the conversation.

"Good evening, Grandfather." He bowed. "Cathal."

"Ah, just in time, Darragh," King Ahren said darkly. "I was about to explain to Cathal the next step in our plan here in Criostal."

"Our plan?" Cathal asked skeptically. He did not like where this was going. Neither did Darragh.

"Cathal, she must wear the crown, and then you must kill her."

"Way to cut to the chase, Grandfather," Cathal said, obviously assuming Ahren was joking.

Darragh, on the other hand, could sense that he was *not*, and looked at Cathal with complete and utter horror, though his half-brother's eyes only landed on their grandfather before him.

"Nobody can wear it but her, but if she wears it long enough to restore balance to the world, and with our marriage binding contract, it will be enough. The crown can be yours—"

"Orlaith may be pig-headed, but I hardly think she is worth murdering, Grandfather—"

Darragh interjected, stunned at the casual admittance from his grandfather. "She is the one?"

Ahren answered, nodding his head in Darragh's direction. "And it has been too long we have suffered without the power of the crown. We once thought we could harness it, for it was your father, Cathal, who devised this plan . . ."

"This plan is absurd!" Cathal's gaze was wide with questions and fear alike. "Father would never agree to such a thing. He only put the bloody thing on to try to make our world a better place. It was without contempt—"

"Enough about your father," Ahren said, not without kindness. "I was afraid you would say that, my sweet boy. I was afraid you would say that and not listen." Extending his hand, he reached for his grandson and heir as if to make peace with him.

Cathal extended his fingers forward and touched him. Ahren's arm went around Cathal's back as they hugged, and before Darragh could step forward to intervene—or know what was going on—his grandfather had placed a golden necklace around his neck with an emerald stone on it.

Breaking apart, Cathal's hand was grasped firmly around the new weight he carried. "What is this, Grandfather?" he asked, his eyes wide in horror.

"Insurance."

"What do you mean?"

"You will marry the Queen of Criostal. You will get the Emerald Crown atop her head, and then you will drive her sword through her heart. It is quite poetic, and the way that things must be done. And regrettably so. I do not take life willingly, but we have no choice."

"Grandfather, this cannot stand—"

Raising a hand, Ahren looked at him, devoid of all the compassion that usually resided within him. "Our world is dying, and this land only remains strong because of her. Because of the power that flows within her."

He pointed to the chain and stone around his heir's neck and said, "If you do not follow through with my duties, if you do not comply, your heart will stop beating, boy."

Darragh was sure he was going to vomit, for the ground began to sway underneath his feet. What was the true reason behind this? Surely, it was not just to get the world back on its own two feet?

Though Cathal did not budge. He stood taller, his gaze filled with betrayal and anger alike. "Then take me now."

Ahren rolled his eyes. "I figured you would say that too, so I think this will entice you." He took a step forward, level with his grandson. "If you disobey me, Darragh will join you in the afterlife. I will ensure it."

"You would not kill your own family!" Cathal's voice was filled with madness. "You raised us! We are your heirs—"

"I will reign eternally with this command, and I will do anything to ensure it." He paused, measuring up to Cathal before turning to Darragh. "The Emerald Crown will be moved tomorrow and be here within the month by the soldiers of Teine. From there, the marriage will commence, and the queen will die."

"You are mad."

"But you will do it."

If the heir to the ashen kingdom had one weakness, it was the life of his bastard brother. To a fault, Darragh knew Cathal would not sacrifice him for the life of one queen. Even if she was incorrigible, she did not deserve to die.

Cathal opened his mouth to protest, but Darragh knew.

Darragh knew he would do it.

CHAPTER 17

CATHAL

The necklace around Cathal's neck was mighty for being so small.

This ball could not come to a close sooner. The music halted in the wee hours of the morning—no queen in sight—and so did Cathal's desire to behave. When he had first entered this ballroom many hours ago, Cathal had been rather impressed with how exquisite the whole thing was.

However, now it was stained.

As was his entire presence here.

As was his entire life.

"What have we done?" Cathal whispered to himself as he walked toward the champagne, pinching his brows. He knew he had onlookers, and typically, he was keen on being exactly what his grandfather wanted.

But right now, he could not stand to think of Ahren.

To kill an enemy was one thing, he supposed. But to kill a queen with the intent of using her for the crown and to save the world? There had to be another way of making things right again. He saw the way she looked at him when he told her that he did not want it. It was earnest, the want for that type of power.

If only he knew how much that type of power could take away, just as it could give.

There was significant desire and understanding in Cathal's relationship with his grandfather. He had heard the account more times than he could count. He could even remember seeing his father, one of his core memories, explaining to him before he left what he was doing.

His father had been under the impression that if he put on the crown, the world would be saved.

But instead, the crown had lied in order to get the essence it needed to keep the lands alive.

For Michael—Cathal and Darragh's father—was not the true ruler of the Isle. And the crown had claimed his soul for the lands.

But they were decaying, and Cathal knew their time was running out.

He supposed his presumed fiancée was right to want to do her duty. And Cathal was not free enough to admit it to his grandfather, but she had a right to be pissed as well.

It had been stolen from her. The details minute.

But it had been stolen, nonetheless.

Running a hand through his dark hair, he held in a pent-up scream. He was at a loss. Was his grandfather insane for suggesting that Darragh and Cathal be responsible for the murder of the queen?

But it was the additional concept that if Cathal did not—

if he let her live . . . It was Cathal's greatest fear. To lose Darragh.

Looking in the mirror, he focused in on himself with a few breaths. It was a coping mechanism Darragh had taught him a few years back, when things became too overwhelming and too much. It was critical to breathe.

So, he did, and then he walked out and slammed the door in the hope of concocting a solution.

And finding a drink.

CHAPTER 18

CATHAL

He walked right into the den of the devil. Newly crowned.

"Grandfather, we must leave while we still can."

Ahren chuckled. He actually chuckled. "Cathal, stop acting as though you are a child. Have you been drinking? Get back to the party; enjoy your bride-to-be."

"Grandfather, this is ridiculous. The Kingdom of Teine does not need a marriage alliance with the Kingdom of Criostal. What we need is—"

"I KNOW DAMN WELL WHAT WE NEED!" King Ahren's voice was laced with darkness so forceful that Cathal took a step back.

Cathal froze, shocked by the outburst from his grandfather.

"You will do as I say, because I am King, and I will punish those who defy me." King Ahren stepped forward, his amber hair glistening in the sunshine of his chambers. Cathal, in this moment, hated how regal he looked. "You know what I did to Darragh all those years ago for breaking the rules?"

Memories flashed before Cathal's gaze as Ahren grabbed his face by the jaw. His long fingernails were cold to the touch and stung as they gripped Cathal's face with anything but kindness.

"I took him in. I have loved him as my own grandson—" He paused, considering his next words carefully so Cathal would be hit by them precisely how he was supposed to be. "But you are my direct line. And if it comes between a choice of what I need from my blood and him, he will suffer more than just that hideous scar."

Launching him backward, Cathal hit the wall with a thump, and all went black.

~

Years Ago

Cathal wandered through the halls of the castle of Teine, an apple in hand, and a mind full of mischief. He had been away at different points in the last few months, training and being schooled on the ways of being a king.

Princely things, one could call them.

But what he most looked forward to, what he dreamt of when he was sad or when he was happy, was this moment. When he could show Darragh how much he had learned, to impress him, and to be reunited with him.

For Cathal, it was always Darragh.

As he rounded the corner, he silently cursed for not grabbing another apple for Darragh. There had been a lovely batch of green ones downstairs on the mantle of the king's quarters, which had been calling to him.

But he simply forgot, for he was too excited to be back with his brother.

As the dark corridor began to lighten with the burning candles, Cathal pushed hard on the heavy oak doors to unveil before him the backs of his brother and grandfather. With a smile plastered on his face, he took a deep breath before he was to launch into a creatively spun tale of his adventures and lessons.

"Darragh, I—"

He paused, a scream nearly exploding from his mouth. The apple hit the floor with a thud, rolling away from him and now the only noise in the room besides his heavy breathing.

Darragh had turned to greet him, though there was no smile that graced his face. Instead, a long bandage covered from the bottom of his nose to his jawline. His face had a black eye, his amber eyes not showing their usual light. The bruising along his jawline was as dark as the walls themselves, and the dark tunic he wore only highlighting the state of things.

The state of him.

"What . . . what happened?" Cathal found himself asking, rushing forward to grab the shoulders of his brother.

His grandfather did not turn around, rather he walked slowly to his throne and then, and only then, turned to face them.

"Darragh learned a lesson," King Ahren said calmly.

"And what lesson was that?" Cathal asked, not taking his eyes off Darragh.

He silently pleaded with him to tell him something, to give

him any inclination as to what had transpired. Certainly, Grandfather would not be capable of such treachery. Surely, Darragh would not have done anything wrong.

"I tried to escape the castle," Darragh said without any ounce of emotion in his voice.

King Ahren sat forward, his pointed ears alert and his expression whimsical, as if this were the first he was hearing such a tale.

"Why would you do such a thing?" Cathal asked slowly, unsure what or who to believe.

Surely, Darragh would not lie to him? They often messed around, were silly, but they never told one another anything but the truth.

"Yes, Darragh, why would you do such a thing?"

"Because I wanted to join you," Darragh whispered, a tear running down the side of his face which was forevermore damaged.

Was it a knife? Cathal wondered. What had Grandfather done to him?

"Darragh—" Cathal started, his hands coming off of his brother's shoulders and balling into fists. Grandfather would pay for this . . .

"Do not blame Grandfather," Darragh said, still looking forward and not directly at Cathal. "This was my chosen punishment."

"How could anyone choose disfigurement?"

"Cathal, you would not understand. Please, let us get some rest. I am sure you had a long journey, and I had a long few months without you."

Cathal's heart sank. This was not what he wanted to hear, not what he expected—

But it was Darragh, and he could tell that whatever the lie was, wherever it was rooted from, it was coming from some form of truth.

And the truth was all Cathal had, so he embraced it.

Extending a hand, he relaxed his own and let Darragh take it.

Cathal never asked him about it again.

CHAPTER 19

ORLAITH

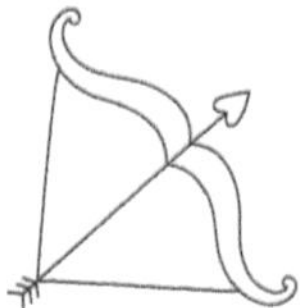

$\mathcal{B}$eing crowned on the sixth day of one's life was a complete and utter bitch.

Orlaith huffed a deep breath to nobody but the Gods who decreed she would know nothing else but the crown, threw her long white hair over her shoulder, and began to saunter toward her bed. It had been a long day—a rather horrible one, in fact—and she could not wait for it to be over.

REENTERING THE BALLROOM, Orlaith went looking for her future husband, only to find his brother.

"I was looking for your other half," she said, approaching him casually. Hopefully, maybe, he had forgotten about seeing her with her sword earlier.

Most improper. She had to quit that behavior. Get back on track. Realign with her goals.

Raising a dark eyebrow, he smiled softly. She realized for the first time that he had a small dimple off the side of his scarred mouth when he smiled. Which, she had learned, was few and far between.

It looked good on him—to smile.

Maybe she should learn to do more of it too.

"I have not seen him in quite some time. I assume he has gone off somewhere of great importance." The sarcasm dripped off his every word, but Orlaith did not miss the fact that his eyes were nonchalantly darting around. Clearly, Darragh was looking for Prince Cathal.

"Interesting," she chided, walking around to the other side of him to get another angle. "Well, if you see him, can you tell him I am looking for him?"

"Whatever for, might I ask?"

"I feel as though we may have gotten off on the wrong foot," she said.

He snorted. "I would say that assumption is fair."

"Do you think, well, do you think he will forgive me?"

An emotion Orlaith was not sure she had seen before swept over his face so quickly that it was soon gone.

"Cathal forgives quicker than anyone else I have ever met. You will be fine. I will pass along your sentiments if I see him before you do."

"Thank you," she said. "I do not know what I expected when I heard the Prince of Teine was coming here, and that he was engaged to be my husband, but certainly, he is unexpected."

"I am not sure what you mean by that," Darragh said, crossing his arms over his body.

"He is . . . most normal."

If Darragh had been drinking something, he definitely would have spit it out. "I will never tell him you said that," he said after a moment to collect himself. "He would be insulted."

Now it was her turn to smile. With a bow, she extended a hand as the music began to pick up once more in the ballroom. "It was my hope to dance with him before I retire for the evening, seeing that this party has gone on for many hours and will continue to do so even long after I am asleep."

Not getting the hint, she stood upright, her hand still extended for the taking. "Will you dance with me, Darragh?"

Frozen, his amber eyes widened, and he blurted, "I do not dance at balls, your majesty. No matter the company I keep."

Feeling bold, she took a step forward, her eyes glinting with raw challenge. "You told me earlier that you will do anything to get what you want, and I told you that I am the same."

"And?" he said, looking down at her. All shock had evaporated from his features, and now he very much matched her own energy.

"And I will get what I want."

Taking her hand, he kissed the top of it lightly. His lips were shockingly soft for how stoic his demeanor was. Overcome with the complex scent of roses and smoke, she lifted her gaze ever so slowly to meet his own. With a light spin, she twirled before him once before he had her chest-to-chest with himself.

Leaning so closely to her that she could see every jagged edge of his scar and every beautiful golden speck in his eyes, he whispered, "Not tonight," before leaving her standing there shocked in his wake.

—

Orlaith dreamt of who she was raised to be, not of who she was.

She dreamt of putting on the crown, as she had many times before.

Except this dream was different.

This was a dream she did not survive.

She knew it the moment her hands touched the gracious object that had caused her life and the world so much pain. The gold was heavier than she anticipated, cold to the touch. It was sucking the life from her in that very moment, but she knew what she had to do.

She knew what she owed her world.

She would do as Michael would do, she decided at that very moment.

Lifting her shaking hands, she heard the voices of the maesters cheering her on. Those sick, disgusting old cretins were cheering on the death of their queen.

If she was not going to die, she would have had their heads.

But it was the other voices that she singled out, telling her not to do it, that were so ominous.

She heard Dealla first, of course. Even Alby. They were telling her to stop, that there must be another way.

"There is no other way!" she shouted back at them, though she was certain they could not hear her.

And then she heard the voice of the scarred elf.

Of Darragh.

It was softer than all of the other voices. Less commanding. She could not tell if Cathal was yelling, or if he was even there to begin with, but she did know that one thing was overcoming her. She was frozen. Her hands trembling violently as the crown was mere inches from the top of her head. This was the closest she had ever come to her destiny. This was the moment she was born for—she could feel it.

Though all she could do in that moment was stare into the deep amber gaze of the elven bastard with the long scar over his face.

And it was destroying her.

That was the only emotion she could register.

Destruction.

Not the crown.

But his amber gaze.

"You do not need to put it on, your Majesty," his voice whispered.

Dealla and Alby were still yelling.

The maesters were still encouraging her.

Yet she found that she did not care.

For there was only Darragh.

CHAPTER 20

ORLAITH

Orlaith woke up.

Decidedly, wine was an evil substance, created by the Gods Just and Mercy to kill the minds of those who enjoyed the joys in life. Or at least, that is what Orlaith told herself this very morning.

She was also convinced the Gods were fucking with her. Trying to destroy her. Maybe they wanted her dead at this point. Why else would they have sent her a dream of fucking Darragh? She nearly heaved. *What was wrong with her?* Her reality was bad enough, engaged to the Prince of Tiene and forced to have *them* at her home for the foreseeable future until this whole performative union nonsense was over.

If it was *ever* to be over and done with.

Sitting up, she reached for the chalice of water Alby had clearly put at her bedside table. After she had returned from sword fighting, she had drank herself into oblivion with wine. It was not the finest coping mechanism, but she had an extremely long day prior and needed to take her mind off of things.

She forgot how much wine it took for an elf to get drunk, for she nearly did not feel anything until she had finished the bottle of red. And all of the other things she had consumed amidst the celebrations. If one could call them that.

And then she had fallen asleep.

And had that horrific dream.

"Gods," she whispered, holding the temple of her head with her fingers. "I am falling apart."

Walking toward the large mirror in her chambers, Orlaith touched the crystalized edges and tried to ponder how to salvage her appearance when Alby strolled in carrying a cup of herbal tea with a girl trailing behind her.

"Where is Dealla?" Orlaith asked the elf with brown hair who was absolutely not her best friend.

After a pause, Orlaith realized this was the truth, though she did not mean it as intentionally mean as it had sounded in her head.

"I do not know, your Majesty. I was sent to retrieve you this morning."

"By whom?" Orlaith half-shouted, her senses becoming fully scented with rage. It was insensible that someone would be commanding her—

"I do not know, your Majesty . . . It was simply a voice that awoke me from my slumber. It was something I had no control over. I simply awoke and knew I was to serve you today in this way."

"Are you playing with me?" Orlaith spat, her face inches from the girl.

The girl—who Orlaith knew she should ask her name, yet could not bring herself to dedicate herself toward one more thing in her absurdly overwhelming life—shirked backward. Orlaith knew her venomous tongue could, and would, sting those who were of soft souls, but she leaned into the one thing that gave her the confidence and prowess to be a queen.

"Sorry, my apologies," Orlaith muttered, trying to muster the energy in this moment to care.

Long fingers wiped down the forefront of her face in exasperation, breathing through all of the stress she had endured since King Ahren had randomly shown up in her library. Her sanctuary.

"I have been going through quite a bit of change the past few days," Orlaith said gently, eager not to unveil weakness but apologetic understanding to the girl.

"I understand, your Majesty," the girl whispered. "I apologize for my response not being adequate. I do not know where Miss Ravayarus is at the moment. I could send for her if you would like her to accompany you for the remainder of the evening."

Orlaith considered it, but felt she could use a moment alone. She did not need Dealla trying to plague her influence this evening as she tried to take in all that she had. She was trying to cope with the situation, and her go-to was normally to go to Dealla. She would serve as the perfect distraction—the perfect person, and maybe the only person—who could wrangle her back to reality and make her see reason.

But based upon their conversation last night, there was no reasoning with Dealla when it came to this. She did not feel like getting scolded again today, for this was something she knew she had to do. It was all for the crown, or the world would fall to ruin. Dealla would tell her, she knew, to damn the world.

But Orlaith could do no such thing, for there was something so deep and impertinent that lay dormant within her until the crown was mentioned. It had taken everything from her: her father's soul, her people's livelihood, and now it demanded to be brought home.

She also had to strategize the regaining of her crown. Where was it located? When she put it on, how long would it take for the Gods to take over and restore all that the continent had lost? What would become of her and her kingdom if she was not the true ruler? She had much to consider, and even though Dealla was her best friend, she knew she could not be distracted.

Dealla was always a distraction.

Smiling to herself as she pushed away the thought of her adventurous friend, Orlaith continued to let the girl dress her for the day. When she was finished, she beckoned for Alby, and they brought her a cup of tea to enjoy.

"What flavor is this?" Orlaith asked Alby.

"Blood orange, my Queen," Alby said. "It is a gift from the Prince Darragh."

Orlaith nearly spit it out. Did he claim the title of prince? Or was this rather Alby being polite?

"He said it is one of his favorite flavors. A delicacy from the Kingdom of Teine."

Despite relishing in the flavors bursting on her tongue,

she spit it out. "You can tell Darragh that I appreciate the gesture, Alby, but the notion is declined."

With a soft and silent smile, Alby took the cup of tea, and Orlaith continued to get ready for her day. But the scent of orange continued to flutter through her senses, and Orlaith found herself craving another sip.

CHAPTER 21

CATHAL

Cathal had awoken on the floor. Alone. Head throbbing. Hand shaking, he had risen and found himself at a loss. Ahren had never laid a hand on him before. But the light had been knocked out of Cathal. He had tried to fight him . . .

As he stood up, head throbbing, Cathal wished someone would lie to him. Tell him this whole venture to Criostal was a mistake. That the world he lived in was not as fucked up as he had just figured out.

The Emerald Crown's diseased touch seemed to spread and taint further than anyone even realized.

So, he rose, not bothering to change out of his clothes, and headed for the one place where he could be lied to. Where he could live a lie. Where he could embrace being the loner that he was.

A tavern.

～

CATHAL STUCK out in the village like a sore thumb. There was no running from his identity, none at all. But it was the whispers, the truth of his position in relation to the queen, that he wished he could escape.

He was used to the crown, used to the drama and rumor-mill that was always created as a result of him merely breathing.

If he sneezed in the courts of home, he would expect to hear rumors of his untimely death. If he kissed the hand of an unmarried elven girl, she was to be his wife. If he drank too much wine and felt the effects, he was a drunkard. Cathal's entire life was rumored, so much so that it was often hard for him to find the line between fact and fiction. Was he a drunk? Was he supposed to marry that girl? Was his death to be untimely?

One thing was to be certain, however, Cathal was completely and utterly fucked. He was to be married to not just the Queen of the Kingdom that rivaled his own, but she was not as intolerable as he had thought.

It was a nightmare, truly.

There had been a moment with her when she had woken up after her power pulsating, where she had been engaged in conversation with him. And he knew it had been real. The images of her then were intelligent, kind, and peaceful. He could see it, the allure that was her.

But the emerald around his neck hung heavy, as did the side of his head where it had connected with the wall.

Rolling his eyes, he continued to stroll toward nothing at all.

This was his favorite activity, after all, not doing much, yet taking everything in. The Kingdom of Criostal was not all that different from his own kingdom, not that he would ever admit that to anyone.

Especially his fiancée.

As he moved to turn a corner, a soft hand touched the crook of his elbow. "Your Majesty," the voice of the young elven boy sounded cautiously. "I do not mean to disrespect, only to welcome you to our kingdom."

Cathal smiled—a part of his job being heir to the ashen throne—and dipped his head in courtesy. "I appreciate that immensely." He leaned forward, his dark hair falling over his gaze casually. "And what is your name? Might I ask."

"Cormac, your Majesty."

"Please, call me Cathal. I do not rule here."

"But you are to marry Queen Orlaith, are you not?"

It took everything within Cathal not to reply sarcastically, but he knew one thing about Orlaith from meeting her —she'd do anything for her kingdom.

He understood that, for he would do anything for his own.

"Yes, I am engaged to marry your queen."

Cormac smiled, his green eyes showing in pure excitement. It was rather humbling in this moment, to see Orlaith be so humanized despite knowing the snarls that came directly from her lips.

"That is just wonderful news. Our queen is so lucky to have you to unite us."

Cathal paused, not thinking of it like that at all.

But he leaned into it.

"I suppose it is such a feat." He bowed once more, bidding Cormac a farewell. "Your queen is lucky to have you as a member of this great kingdom."

Cormac returned the bow, and Cathal was on his way once more to embrace the kingdom he supposed he was to unite and call his own. Maybe there would be a way around the fate, a way to break the emerald stone's curse that sat with him . . .

But first he was to finish his drink. And forget.

CHAPTER 22

ORLAITH

Orlaith left her chambers, saw the rising in the sky, and could feel that something was completely and utterly wrong.

Getting up, she did not even bother to go back for Alby in the chambers over or call for guards. She could feel a tugging, as if the light that resided within her was yanking her toward some great darkness.

But it was more than darkness—Orlaith could tell that whatever had awoken her was pure evil.

Before she knew it, she was running through the halls of her crystalized castle. Suddenly, all aspirations of the day were dead and gone to her. She knew nothing but the pure terror that tore at her. Manic, her turquoise eyes struggled to land on one face for more than a second. All she needed to see to move onto the next person was the fact that none of them were Dealla.

Where was Dealla?

With every step, she could feel a wave of nausea set over her senses. Orlaith had never been nervous before, never been afraid or confused. She was fearless. She was brilliant. And at this moment—right now—she was terrified.

"Dealla?" she shouted, passing more concerned castle-goers and members of her court as she tore on.

"My Queen?" she heard someone ask, their voice far away.

It was not the voice of Dealla.

She did not answer.

"Is that the queen?" She heard someone exclaim, their voice far away too. They were not Dealla either.

She did not answer, finding herself unable to care for even a moment that there were foreigners still in her home from the evening prior.

She was on a mission to go to Dealla's room, for that was the only place she had not checked. It was so unlike Dealla to disappear, to not want to be a part of the action of the evening. And they had a horrible fight.

Why had she not gone sooner? Why would she abandon her friend as such? Her *best* friend.

Orlaith's ability to be stubborn was as concerning as it was admirable at times. She was a queen first and foremost, but she never flexed it in the face of her friends. The Maesters? Absolutely. But never Dealla.

Never Dealla.

She realized, in that exact moment, that she had been just that: too stubborn. She should have listened to her own heart.

Something was, in fact, very wrong. And she was the only one who seemed to notice.

"Dealla?" Orlaith called again as she made her way to the large door, and with hands trembling, she pushed with all of her might.

Eyes adjusting to the change in light, Orlaith moved her mouth to open it and call out her friend's name when she paused.

Then, she was on her knees.

She was crawling.

She was sobbing.

She was shaking.

She was moving as fast as she could.

She was not moving fast enough.

She was not sure she was breathing.

She was sure she was covered in the pool of blood she had just crawled through.

She was not sure how this could be.

She was not sure *when* this happened.

She was not sure how Dealla could be . . . *gone*.

But there she was, lying in a pool of blood so richly red that it could only belong to her.

And Orlaith screamed.

She screamed for her friend.

She screamed for the horror.

She screamed for herself.

Because if Dealla was lost, then all light was lost. She was not whole—

Voice raw, she crumbled into herself. She felt hands on her, not caring to look who they belonged to.

She was falling. She was nothing.

And then light flared, and the shrieking started.

Maybe, after all this, she was a monster rather than a queen.

CHAPTER 23

CATHAL

Two weeks later

Despite his good-natured conversation at the tavern two weeks ago with that elf named Cormac, Cathal wanted to vomit in the presence of his betrothed.

He still bloody hated this place.

Orlaith was utterly divine—that much could not be ignored—but it was her soul that Cathal was convinced was utterly black.

So much for being the Queen of Light.

She jested him at every turn. Blocked him at every opening he thought he might be able to crack through to get to her at the core. He could not find himself even rubbing his own eye without some sort of detached and irritated comment that somehow managed to insult every piece of what made him . . . well, him. If he was not so appalled by her in every way, he would have been impressed.

Despite what Orlaith thought, he was not a klutz, and he could sense that these extremely viable rude tendencies of hers were not out of her heart truly being black. Some centripetal force was driving her to be so combative, especially with him. He just needed to find her motivations, what made her tick, and how to stop being so thrown off by her backhanded comments.

He thought he was quick of the mouth, but it turns out that she was lightning fast.

Despite the acidity that rose in his throat at the mere thought of having to be wed to this creature, he truly became ill thinking what his grandfather had demanded of him nights before.

Her head on a spike.

No, no. He did not want that. Even if, at the moment, it was rather tempting—

"Are you even paying attention to a word I say, Prince Cathal?"

There. There was her voice again, so filled with judgement. How dare he let his mind wander for even a moment . . .

"I did not go anywhere. I was merely plotting how to dodge your next comment."

And how not to kill you, he stopped himself from adding.

"Good luck with that," she said without giving him a glance. Her profile was set straight ahead as they walked down the aisle in practice for this very evening.

King Ahren had demanded that they be wed.

And somehow, he had gotten Orlaith to agree, though

his grandfather had been kind enough to instate that they were to grieve first for the death of Orlaith's close friend.

Death was a kind word for what happened to her, Cathal had supposed. It was completely and utterly foul, a display of absolute power by someone's account. And they had gotten out of the castle without as much as a sniff on their trail.

It was madness.

And now Cathal sat here and walked with the white-haired elf to both of their dooms. How could you tell someone that their means to an end was your prerogative to murder them for power?

He was not sure who was more positively fucked, but he could not help but think it was him.

Despite all that she had been through in the last two weeks.

"You know, I could try harder to get out of this," Cathal muttered lowly in her ear. He knew it irritated her without even knowing her long because elves had such natural precise hearing.

"Do I frighten you?" she said, turning her face to meet his. Though Cathal did not break from her, refusing to back down despite the fact that their noses were nearly touching.

Her turquoise gaze blazed with indignation and challenge, and he rose to meet her with a devilish smile.

"Not in the slightest."

"That will change," she growled before whipping her head the other direction.

"Will it? I would like to see your best—" he started before they arrived at the end of the aisle already, breaking as they would this evening to take their vows to one another's kingdoms and unite the Isle in the name of a lie.

"You bore me with your attempt to match me in stride," she whispered lowly.

Cathal opened his mouth to reply, but shut his jaw instead. It seemed he would have forever to argue with the queen. Why continue when he knew he had lost? He would keep losing too. This whole relationship was won by her, despite the fact that he feared deeply it would end in his hands covered in blood.

Instead, he settled on a grunt. Discreet to all the eyes on them, yet distinctively satisfied in losing this round between them.

"Checkmate," she growled with a wink.

He nearly lost it before he felt a hand come to his shoulder, that familiar calming presence that nobody else on the Isle could emulate. Darragh.

"Everything going swimmingly, brother?" Darragh hissed.

Cathal did not turn his head to see if his wife-to-be was looking at Darragh. Instead, he merely turned to face his brother and put both arms on his shoulders. "I need to get out of here. Please get me out of here—"

Darragh snorted, his red hair dancing in the light that shone onto the front of the chapel where they stood. "You know I cannot do that, Caw."

"She is insane. She is bloody nuts."

"Is she?" Darragh said with a smile, his eyes wandering to where Orlaith now stood on the other side of the cathedral with some of the Criostal servants. "She looks harmless."

"The wicked mouth on her—" Cathal paused, careful not to put too much emotion into his words, knowing she was probably listening and would wield it against him later. "Even you would have a hard time quelling that fire, brother. I am happy to claim her insane. Maybe then Grandfather can chop this emerald necklace off of me and—"

Cathal knew it was true too. Darragh had a way about him that was settling, yet unsettling. He was darkness embodied in natural beauty. His red hair was cropped and most uncommon for an elf, and a rugged scar cut unkindly across his face was utterly unlike most elves Cathal had met in his lifetime.

But that was a part of why Darragh was so enchanting.

Because he was *different*.

And because no flames—no matter how hot and dangerous they were—would scare him away. He was born of fire and ash, and Cathal knew with every fiber of his being that Darragh would rather burn the world down than give up on anything.

"May we get a pint? A glass of wine in my chambers?" Ignoring his comment. Per usual. Wonderful. Cathal was positively fucked. It was now certain; for Darragh seemed to avoid every opportunity to discuss the inevitable.

Cathal was going to have to commit treason to keep him alive. There was no way that Darragh was going to accept this without a fight. All Cathal could keep doing was reminding him of the stakes until he broke.

Darragh plucked his brother's hands off his shoulders as he pondered the question. Looking around, his amber eyes met Cathal's with a menacing smirk that spoke silently that he was up to absolutely no good.

And instead of answering, he merely accepted a hand. And then they were off.

~

THEY LEFT Orlaith to her own devices, and Cathal was rather grateful for the silence. He knew he was being rather unreasonable: Orlaith was not insane. She was merely holding it together, confused and broken. He had been there a few times himself, but that was what it felt like to be sitting and staring at your own reflection: completely and utterly insane.

Maybe that was why they struggled so much with one another. Why they jested at every single turn . . .They were too bloody similar, and when they looked at one another, it was like looking in the mirror.

And like most, they both clearly did not like whatever looked back at them.

The pouring of wine snapped Cathal back to reality, seeing Darragh lifting the golden chalice and bringing it to Cathal's hands. The liquid was room temperature, clearly fermented well.

If there was one thing the Kingdom of Criostal did well, it was their wine.

"She is hurting more than you know," Darragh whispered.

Why was he always so right? It was maddening.

"I can not let myself feel bad for her, Darragh. There is too much hanging in the balance for me to simply feel bad."

"It is a human emotion," Darragh attempted.

"I am not human, if you have not noticed, dear brother." He pointed to the tips of his ears. "And neither are you."

"I am more human than you," Darragh whispered softly, as if the winds here would tell on him for being as such.

Cathal knew what he meant; Darragh was not fully royal.

"It is OK to be sad, Cathal. We are allowed to feel empathy."

"It will make it harder when I have to do it."

There it was. The unspoken words Cathal had been avoiding these last two weeks. The thing his grandfather had demanded and cursed him to do.

Kill Orlaith.

Or kill Darragh.

The choice was simple, even though it was everything but.

"I have been in her library . . .searching . . ."

Cathal held up a hand. He did not want to do this dance. For whatever reason, Darragh was ill-content with the thought of Cathal murdering the Queen of Criostal. He was more against it than Cathal was, at least on the surface. Here it was, though, Darragh starting to crack open. He had many layers, not unlike Orlaith herself.

But when Cathal was alone at night, and he thought about taking a dagger to her chest . . .

Well, the first time he had thought of it, he had vomited.

So, it had gone swimmingly.

"I do not want to speak of this," he whispered, taking a rather large sip of his red wine. "You are not leaving me."

"Her life is far more valuable than mine, brother."

Cathal stood in an instant, red wine splattering to the floor as the chalice clamored against the marble beneath his feet. "You. Are. Not. Leaving. Me."

Darragh did not understand.

Instead, he took a step toward his brother. "You are not going to ruin yourself by doing this. I will keep searching until my last breath."

"So, you are searching," Cathal whispered, rather victorious. "Or hers."

"It will be mine. Open your eyes, brother. She is the only chance this world has."

With a snarl, Cathal moved to attack his brother. To shove him against something, to draw swords and duel—

But he was resigned. And Darragh was walking out the door.

All sounds were devoid but the wine which dripped on the floor around him.

CHAPTER 24

ORLAITH

Orlaith was not sure how many times she had thrown up in the last two weeks.

White hair had been plastered to the nape of her neck, and although she was an elf—and therefore nearly impervious to all diseases which could kill humans—she was unconvinced that she was not on the verge of death.

Dealla was gone . . .

Her hands shook uncontrollably even now as she tried to cross them in front of her torso. They had been so blood-soaked and crusted quickly . . . Orlaith was in shambles.

But she held her head high, because that was what queens did. Even now, with the memory haunting.

"Your Majesty." She heard a voice behind her, filled with angst and concern alike.

She did not turn, but she did speak. "What is it, Prince Cathal?"

"I was merely checking in on you . . . when . . ."

"When what?"

"When I thought you might need to talk to someone. You do not have to be OK."

She took three deep breaths.

In and out.

In and out.

In and out.

"What is with the change of heart, Prince Cathal? Do you have anything of value to say to me? I am due to meet with the Maesters in order to address the th-threat that entered our domain two weeks ago, and I do not have time to—"

She paused. Cut off by the hand which was now touching her bare shoulder. She could not believe this. Could not believe he would have such audacity to—

"You know," Cathal whispered, so low in her ear that nobody else in the hall could hear it. They would merely think this was ornamental, a romantic display of a prince engaged to a queen, that it was out of duty. But Orlaith could hear it in his voice. It was actual desperation. It was actual concern. It was friendship. Ally-ship. "Queens do not have to be so strong all the time. You are still covered in the blood of your friend. If you need to get out of that room at any time, just say the word, and I will do it."

"Why are you being nice to me?" she asked, her voice shaky for what felt like the first time in her life.

"Because I respect you, believe it or not. And I might have had a nice conversation with my brother. Very awe-inspiring."

"Klutz," she said with a huff.

"That is the spirit."

Without giving him another glance, she continued to walk toward the Maesters room. As she entered, they bowed ceremoniously. She could tell Cathal was no more than a foot behind her, except she felt no need to comment on it. She would never tell him this, but in this moment, she was grateful.

She needed a friend, now more than ever.

And she guessed Cathal would have to do. Since her only friend was gone.

King Ahren's voice cut through the air like a knife as she took a seat at the head of the table. "My dear queen, might I start by saying what a terrible loss this is for us all."

Orlaith bit her tongue. This was not the time to lose her shit in front of the maesters. So, she did what she did best. She ignored him.

Grunting with disapproval, King Ahren continued, "Clearly, these castles are unsafe. Clearly, the Kingdom of Criostal is unsafe. It is my prerogative that we move the queen and prince to the Kingdom of Tiene as soon as possible in order to provide them with a safe and happy union."

Orlaith swore Cathal's mouth was agape, even though she continued to refuse to make eye contact with him.

Three Maesters spoke at once. "King Ahren, with all due respect, I do not believe that is appropriate. May we remind you that Queen Orlaith is the queen, and Prince Cathal is merely that . . . A prince."

"Offense taken," Cathal whispered under his breath.

Fighting a smirk, Orlaith spoke clearer than she had since

she found the body of her friend. "I will not be leaving the confines of my castle, King Ahren, with all due respect. I am set on a path to find whoever did this too—" The words would not leave her mouth, but there it was again, that hovering presence over her shoulder.

Cathal.

King Ahren looked positively lethal. To be defied by the Maesters was out of his control, but to be defied by the queen herself was unacceptable. With a snarl, he opened his mouth for a rebuttal, when suddenly the doors to the chambers opened, and a dark wind whispered across their faces.

The candles went out.

Orlaith could hear a woman screaming.

Everyone had covered their ears.

A cold breeze whispered over their bodies.

Freezing.

Icy.

Filled with death.

Orlaith tried to lift her head, which had bowed against her will, and then she saw it.

A dark hooded figure, a hand so dark and imminent with death, holding a dagger. She knew what the creature was before he fully came into vision. She had spent so many years reading fairytales. The word was so vehemently trying to make its way off her tongue that she ended up saying nothing at all.

With a scream that cut through the air like broken glass, the creature plunged that dagger into the heart of King Ahren. And the world erupted and disintegrated all at once.

He stumbled at first. His gaze went straight to Cathal, who was frozen with fear and shock.

And then he fell to the floor slowly.

But there was no way he could die. Not unless—

Unless there was some darker magic at play.

Unless there was something Orlaith did not understand.

That creature had murdered the King of Tiene in cold blood. And now he was gone, the flash of darkness minute but very much there. He had disappeared into thin air.

And now Orlaith was standing, dragging Cathal with her as the screams continued to rip throughout the halls.

CHAPTER 25

They were death incarnate; that much was to be certain.

And they were oh so very angry.

The King of Anord was draped in complete darkness; it flowed off of him audibly. The tendrils of these dark whispers curled in likeness to air around the girl he had murdered not weeks before.

She had seen him, therefore she had to die.

It was admirable, the way she had fought back. Her dark skin and long light hair illuminated seconds before the candles were blown out by his dark power, an image so beautiful that he almost felt remorseful nobody would write the song of how she died. For they would never know. He thought the tale would have been lovely, even though he did not think at all.

Lifting a hand, he unveiled the scene of the Queen of

Light begging for her friend to return, even though she knew there was no essence left in her friend's body.

The Gods Just and Mercy had no power of Anord. The wraiths were in full strength on the continent. The humans and elves of the Isle would do well to remember it, for Anord believed himself to be the master of it all.

He thought the same, as he had driven the blade through the heart of the king. A deed which needed to be done years prior, though Anord had been waiting waiting waiting for the right moment.

For this day.

Cracking his phantom hands, he sat back in his throne and called his children back to him. They would fly, faster than the wind and lighter than the sun's touch on flowers.

And then their real work would begin.

CHAPTER 26

DARRAGH

Darragh had his arms on Cathal as he tried to run to wherever was safe.

If safe was even a place.

"CATHAL!" Darragh screamed among the chaos. "CATHAL, WE NEED TO MOVE!"

It had seemed as if the wraiths—Darragh swore that was what they were—had gone faster than they had come. But it did not mean this place was safe. And Cathal needed to be at a safe place.

He was the King of Teine.

Sobs wracked Cathal as Darragh tried to drag him from the council chambers. Cathal was stronger than Darragh had anticipated.

Unsurprisingly, he was not used to holding back his brother in such a state.

"Cathal—" Darragh groaned, once more dragging him from the room as his king and brother sobbed.

As he rounded the corner to drag Cathal back to his chambers—the only safe place he could think of in a pinch—an ethereal hand reached toward him. "Princeling," the voice said, so unusually calm despite all that was going on. "Prince Cathal, please come with me."

A flash of white hair. A soft burst of light.

It was Queen Orlaith.

"Your Majesty," Darragh huffed. "He is in shock, your Majesty."

"It is going to be OK," Orlaith hummed. "Into my chambers."

Putting a glowing hand on Cathal, he went with her, to Darragh's shock. She locked the door as they entered and stood at the back of it, chest heaving slightly.

"What was that?" Darragh whispered as he laid Cathal down on the bed, his eyes closed and his breathing slowing.

"He is going to sleep," she muttered, seeming very far away.

"Did you do this to him?"

"I may not be able to pelt my enemies with wind blasts, but my light has quite a few useful properties."

Darragh snorted, despite his best efforts. "He is gone."

"And you are free of those confines then, I suppose."

Darragh opened his mouth to retort something regarding how Ahren had taken him in as a bastard, but he knew deep down she was right. "I am sorry your friend is lost as well."

Despite whatever hung between the three of them, he did not want her to think him heartless. He had a difficult relationship with his grandfather, and although shock reverberated through him, he was not surprised to find himself devoid of the usual grief that overcame anyone who lost family before their very eyes.

Orlaith's turquoise eyes flashed sad, and Darragh rather sympathized with this human side of the queen. He wondered how much longer he would have it before she disappeared from him, and he was left once more with the queen who was a combatant at every turn.

"We cannot dwell now. We must strategize."

"Are you thinking of leaving?"

"I do not think it would be wise to stay here."

Surprise filtered through him. "But your people need you—"

"My people need the lands to be restored, Darragh. I am no use to them if I continue to let the Emerald Crown sit there and not be used for its true power. The Gods cannot fester this land when my birthright is on the line!"

Darragh paused.

One, she had used his name so casually. He liked the way it sounded on her lips.

Two, she was right. They could not sit here when an enemy had burst through the doors.

But it was the third thought that brewed in his mind that he could not escape from.

"What do you mean your birthright is on the line?"

Orlaith froze, that cold demeanor sweeping over her again.

He had lost her.

Great.

"Exactly what I said. I intend to wear the crown."

Darragh's mouth fell agape.

But he understood.

It was duty.

And he got that more than anything.

"Get some rest," he muttered softly, working with this situation delicately. He could not afford to have her mistrusting him, for it seemed as though Cathal for all his annoyances had cracked through some part of her that was reasonable and fiercely loyal. "I will take the first watch."

She paused, skeptical clearly. "And?"

"And then when you and Caw awaken, we will take you to what is rightfully yours."

It was an omen of death, one which he knew he would come to regret. But he had time then to get himself a plan, a plan to save everyone.

Ahren would not win. Darragh would not allow it.

CHAPTER 27

*I*t started small.

Rebellions and war—they always did.

The wraiths had crept in while the others were off intruding on the Queen of Light. They were quiet, even now. Their shadows stayed within an arm's length, afraid to trigger the people of the ashen kingdom and alert their king that there was something amiss.

Well, the wraith thought with a smirk, *their new king.*

Teine had been compromised. With no monarch home for two weeks, they had time to do what they needed to do: infiltrate.

Oh, this is going to be grand fun, the wraith hissed. *Great fun, indeed.*

PART II
LEANNÁN

CHAPTER 28

DARRAGH

Orlaith had been pacing. And Darragh, for all it was worth and for all that he had begun to learn about her, realized this was not something that came naturally to her. She was not one to be rattled.

He was worried, though he tried not to smile as he watched the Isle famous Queen of Criostal try to problem-solve.

To her disadvantage, at this moment, they had many problems.

"How did they get in?" she was asking nobody in particular, staring out the window of the room they had barricaded themselves in last night. "And why kill Dealla? She was not a threat to anyone politically—nor was she a public figure. Merely a member of the court."

She paused, pondering. Darragh withheld a snort. It was so rare to see monarchs in such a light.

Especially one as fearsome in person as the queen, and as ambiguous in the shadows.

"Clearly, King Ahren was a target of this whole play. It made sense to kill him."

"Watch your tongue," Darragh half-growled. "That is my grandfather."

Orlaith whipped her white head around, eyes blitzing, but also soft in a contradictory sort-of-way. "I am sorry." She glanced down at the sleeping Cathal, and the hard line of her mouth softened. "I just do not know what could have caused this—"

"Do you mean it?" Darragh found himself asking, despite his best efforts to remain neutral.

"I do," she half-barked, eyes not leaving Cathal. "I know what it is to lose family."

"You were quite young?" Darragh asked, even though he knew the answer.

Everyone knew the Queen of Criostal was crowned on her sixth day of life. He did not know why he did not say it out loud, other than some part of him felt like he needed to hear her say it. Maybe it would allow him to understand her better.

"I do not remember a moment in my life where I was not a queen." She paused, her gaze filled with mischief and wonder. "You know, I was only six days old when the crown became mine."

Darragh chuckled, trying to lighten the mood. "I do not remember a time in my life where I was not a bastard."

She smiled. She *actually* smiled.

"You are not so bad," she whispered, moving her hand to

touch the top of Cathal's dark hair. The act was rather motherly, though Darragh knew Orlaith was nothing even close to a mother. "He is not so bad, either."

"He is going to struggle with this," Darragh said softly. "He was a lot closer to my grandfather than he will even care to admit."

"He will survive," she said in deference.

"How can you know?" Darragh breathed out. "How can you know when you do not even know him? That is quite the assumption to make."

The Queen of Criostal looked up at him, turquoise eyes back to their familiar sea-glass fire. Darragh noticed, not for the first time, that Orlaith wore her emotions in her eyes. It could all be read if one just looked.

"Because I have lived through much worse, and I know you have too. And look at us now."

"You have lost a lot of people then?"

"Are you forgetting my best friend was murdered in cold blood two weeks ago?"

"I could never forget such a thing," Darragh said, knotting his hands behind his back so he could ignore how he somehow wanted to reach out and brush the white hair that tumbled down over her shoulder. He had to speak carefully, choose his words carefully, to risk igniting that fire within her.

"Sorry," she said, turning to look out the window again. "I tend to come off so harsh, but it is my nature to always be on defense."

"And why are you telling me this?" he asked, curious why she was opening up in bursts.

"Because once he wakes up," she said, gesturing to Cathal, "we are going to your kingdom, and you are going to help me get my crown."

A crashing sound came from the hallway.

And Orlaith was up and moving before Darragh had a chance to voice that he was going to check it out.

With a grunt, he took off after her. Her hands were reaching for the longsword strapped across her back, a piece which he had come to associate with her.

And her strength.

The door opened, and Darragh followed her silently. Looking left to right, he saw nothing. Though the crystal hallways had remained dark, as if the stones themselves were dimmed by what had happened here.

What had happened to Dealla and Ahren.

He shuddered, dreaming for this nightmare to end.

And then Orlaith took off down the hallway.

Swearing, he chased after her. Immediately, he was self-conscious of his feet pattering on the floor lightly, whereas she was utterly soundless. Damn his nature. It was soft enough that he knew she would not notice, for nobody ever noticed. But he noticed. Every little imperfection. He always did.

As they rounded the corner, Orlaith paused and clearly listened for any changes in the wind. And then they both heard something, their ears picking up and their senses on high alert.

Not realizing they were next to a doorway, Darragh found himself grabbed by the long fingers of the Queen of Criostal and shoved into the room with force. Gasping for breath, Darragh found himself pinned against the wall as Orlaith put a beautifully delicate finger to his own lips.

"Do not make a sound," she mumbled. "I think I heard someone coming."

"You are the one making a—"

Her full hand came over his mouth. And he almost felt like biting the palm of her hand . . . But it was the look in her eyes that made him stop. The air was thrumming around them, as if it were lit up by candles. He looked below Orlaith's collarbones to see if it was her own light making the brightness in the dark between them, but it was to no avail. Her turquoise eyes were alight with mischief and life, the heavy grief that had consumed her the last weeks gone. He even felt his own grief lift from himself as he gazed upon her.

They were electric, heirs in their own right from oppositional kingdoms, yet completely and utterly one.

Leaning closer, she furrowed her brows as if lost in thought. He nearly gasped at her proximity, and the complete masterful detail which was every aspect of her face. She was carved from something greater than he had anticipated: maybe Just and Mercy themselves.

This felt different from their time outside the tavern, for that had been fear as much as it had been a battle of fun. This was intimate. This was terrifying in another way. One Darragh was not sure he understood completely.

He wanted to tell her it was OK to let her light shine, that she had nothing to fear.

Not with Cathal.

Not with him.

But that was not true, for the necklace around Cathal's

neck told a different story entirely. Darragh was no truth teller, but he could not find the words to warn her.

As she opened her lips as if to break the lightened silence between them, the door which had closed behind them opened. It was none other than Orlaith's servant Alby, who stood with a pot of tea.

They gasped, bowing, and rapidly apologizing to their queen for barging in.

As they walked back to where Cathal lay sleeping, Darragh could not help but smirk. For it was he who had made the Queen of Criostal blush.

CHAPTER 29

CATHAL

Cathal was awake before he was awake.

His eyes were closed. He could swear he heard a peaceful conversation between Darragh and Orlaith, and he tried to wish himself back into his stupor.

When he opened his eyes—which he did moments later—he knew he would have to relive everything that had happened, and that he would be thrown into his fate. The fate he had never thought would come. The fate he never wanted to come.

He was the King of Teine.

And his grandfather was dead.

So, he closed his eyes once more and wished he may stay sleeping forevermore.

Cathal did not know how long he continued to lie with his eyes closed. He reckoned Darragh knew he was, for Darragh knew everything.

He rolled over a few times, groaning inadvertently without much effort, and continued to play this role in limbo before he was forced to accept his fate.

Just a few more minutes of silence before he would be forced to reconcile with the violence.

So, he closed them again, though he could sense they knew he was awake.

Cathal eventually opened his eyes to see the Queen of Criostal seated at the foot of his bed, reading a book.

And suddenly he wished he were very much asleep once more.

"Cathal," she whispered after a few heartbeats of silence. "Darragh will be glad to see you awake."

"Where is he?" Cathal asked, his voice rawer than he anticipated. "Where is my brother?"

"He is scouting the castle, making rounds and accounting for what has happened in the last few hours."

Cathal visibly sagged as he sat upright. Darragh was OK. That was all that mattered.

"I am to alert the Maesters when he returns that we are leaving. The three of us. Tonight."

It took a second for her words to process, and instead of commenting, he only said, "You are wearing pants?"

Orlaith looked down at herself, so different from her

usual flower or gem-ridden outfits, and laughed. "They are called leathers. Can females not wear leathers?"

"I have never seen a royal female ordain something so—"

"Practical?" she finished for him with a smirk. "Honestly, klutz, I am shocked this is your sticking point. You have been through quite an ordeal, and honestly, the only thing you have concern about is the fact that I am wearing leathers and a black tunic like a man—"

"No," Cathal said with a breath. "You look brave. That is all."

She paused, her lips parted in surprise, and before she had a chance to answer, Darragh strode through the doorway. He had changed as well, looking like a dark nightmare in pairing to the queen.

Upon seeing his brother, he rushed forward, amber eyes glowing with hope and sadness alike. "You are awake. I will not ask if you are OK, but—"

"I am *fine*," Cathal replied sternly. This was his duty. This was what it meant to be a royal, to put on a face in front of everyone, despite what was going on inside your heart. "You know as well as I do the complicated relationship that we had with Grandfather, and although I was . . . overcome at his death, I understand my role in all of this."

Darragh leaned forward, concern etching across his face. "Just because she is here," he said, whispering and gesturing toward Orlaith, "does not mean you have to be strong. It is OK to be upset—"

"I said I am *fine*, Darragh."

Darragh flinched, and Cathal could have sworn his own heart split down the middle. He hated pushing Darragh away like this, but if he was to survive this, he would have to deal with it later.

"When do we leave?" he asked Orlaith.

"As soon as I talk to the Maesters and inform them of our plans. I will be leaving someone in charge of Criostal in our stead, but I need them to be aware of my location."

"Why does it matter? You are the queen; you can do as you please," Cathal said with a half-smile, trying to will himself back to normal heavily.

Orlaith paused after taking a few strides toward the door. As she looked back, her white hair tumbled over her shoulder and swung freely over the top of her leather pants. "It is a common misconception, my *King*, that rulers have to rule alone. I may despise them and anyone else in my way, but if Dealla taught me one thing . . ."

She paused again, and Cathal nearly fell over at the display of emotion on her face. She had lost too. And it was hurting her more than she let on.

He understood.

"If Dealla taught me one thing," she said, "it is to take all the liberties you can, but to let people help you."

And with that, she grabbed her longsword sitting by the side of the door, strapped it to her back, and left the room without another word.

Darragh sat down upon her leaving, as if he could finally bear to wear his emotions without her in the room.

"Can you feel the power of the gem?"

"I fucking hate emeralds," Cathal whispered, leaning backward against the pillow. "I think that is the intrinsic difference between Orlaith and me. She wants the crown of these damn cursed stones so badly, but she does not know how evil they truly can be . . ."

"They are not evil by nature, Caw," Darragh said sadly. "I take it that you feel the same weight of the curse?"

"It has not left me, not for a fleeting moment." Cathal tried to ignore the intrusive thoughts his dreams had left him. He had envisioned over and over again what was impending between him and the queen. The death. Could he do it? Could he be the one to lift the blade against the Queen of Criostal?

He was not sure, the more time he spent with her. The more humanity he saw. Frankly, he was not sure if he could ever take a life, lest one that he had begun to trust and befriend.

"You are thinking so loudly I can hear it from here," Darragh whispered sadly.

"I am trying to not think at all. Any tips?" Cathal began to stand, trying to orient himself. Anything to stop his thoughts from wandering.

"I find in my life I have discovered a lot of things, Cathal, but turning off my thoughts? I could only dream of having such power."

CHAPTER 30

ORLAITH

She walked down the hallway of her castle, sword strapped to her back, and hair billowing down her back wildly. The Maesters would not recognize her when she entered her council chambers; that much was certain. She had forever been the young queen, born into her role.

Now she looked like she had mastered it.

ORLAITH STOOD in front of the Maesters in the council chambers and commanded their attention. Literature, Stars, Medicine, Horses, Farming, Borders, and Advising all sat up straight, their violet robes in familiar matching unison. Except the difference was tonight they listened to her, rather than telling her their waking thoughts.

She explained it. She explained it *all*.

The murder of Dealla: the feeling of the blood on her

hands, the loss she felt, the horror that someone or something had stepped into her home and deliberately mutilated someone with such a gorgeous soul.

The murder of the king. She was just, and she was honest. She reminded the Maesters of her origins, the fact that the world was suffering because King Ahren thought himself to be just and honorable. However, nobody deserved to die like that.

The Maesters listened, they pondered, and they said nothing as she carried on for upwards of an hour.

When she finished, Orlaith put her hands on her hips and suddenly wished for a glass of cold water.

But she said nothing, only looking at them for an answer, for the promise that they would do what was necessary once again.

That they would rule in her stead, do as she would do, and protect her people while she went to retrieve the thing she had been promised by the King of Teine.

Well, the old King of Teine.

To her surprise, it was the Maester of Horses that spoke first, his voice quiet and filled with the good-natured smile which danced on his lips. "My Queen, you're going to need some horses."

And for the first time in her entire life, Orlaith smiled back at the Maesters and thanked them for their service. She had won. And she only hoped that this was the beginning of a long streak of luck.

Just and Mercy knew she was going to need it.

~

CATHAL CAUGHT her outside of the chambers. He was leaning against the wall of crystals nonchalantly.

It was annoying.

Especially since she knew he was hurting as badly as she was, and he was just as skilled at putting on the mask.

"Do you need something?" she asked, trying to keep disinterest out of her voice. She supposed she was in a good mood, so she did not mind asking.

"Looking for purpose, something I am sure you are familiar with."

"Did you find it?" she asked, unable to stop herself before this banter resumed between them.

"No," he said, touching the golden and emerald necklace slung around his neck.

Was it new? She was rather perceptive and would recognize anything emerald as a symbol of herself. He would not—

"How did you expect our wedding day would have gone?" His question cut through her thoughts like a knife through air.

"Why does it matter?" she asked, unable to keep the annoyance out of her voice. There he went again. Ruining the conversation between them.

"You know you still signed a contract to Teine in exchange for the crown."

She could not keep the surprise out of her voice. "Really, you are going to hold a contract over my head?"

But she had signed it in the hours following King Ahren coming to her library to initiate the proposal between them.

Cathal took a step forward down the hallway, nearly

crushing her against the crystal walls. "You forget that if you put on the crown alone, and you are not who you think you are, you will die without my marriage."

She scoffed. "It is not death I am afraid of. The Maesters approved of me leaving. They are going to run my kingdom as they did before I was crowned."

Orlaith swore she saw him flinch in a panic, but it must have been the trick of the light.

"The land needs someone who is going to be a ruler of the ages, someone the crown cannot control. You have a better shot if you put it on with me at your side."

"You are coming with me, right?" She paused, her irritation building that this was even a conversation they were having.

Why in the name of the Gods was he so damn infuriating?

"And why do not you put it on?" she asked, her voice nearly trembling with rage. How dare he hold this over her?

"I will not go anywhere near that thing. It took my father from me."

"And whose fault is that?" she spat before she immediately retracted. Cursing, she whispered, "I am sorry—"

"No, you are not," Cathal whispered, suddenly very far away. "You are not sorry at all. And why should you be?"

"Cathal—" she said softly. "Cathal, do not walk away from me."

"I am going to gather the rest of my things," he said without turning around. "I will meet you at the carriage. I am going home."

She paused. Did he just say he was . . .

With a smirk, he turned, his index finger touching the emerald necklace around his neck once more. "Are you coming? There is a lot out there, and it will be dangerous."

Orlaith paused. To what was he referencing? But before she had a chance to ask, he was gone.

CHAPTER 31

CATHAL

Cathal did not know if he was ever going to have the guts to tell her what he knew he should: Ahren had the goal of killing her, and if he did not, Darragh would die.

If he could postpone the annulment of their engagement, maybe he could figure it out. He was afraid that their separation would not only hurt Teine, being that he figured Orlaith was the one to save them all, but that it would be enough of a break in Ahren's agreement to kill Darragh.

And despite how much he was coming to respect the queen and how much he loved the Isle, nothing was more important to Cathal than Darragh.

He would go to the ends of the lands for him, take a dagger to the heart for him. That is what it meant to be family. True family.

"You OK, Caw? You thinking again?" Darragh asked, his voice filled with humor.

"My mind is very heavy. I have not quite figured out how to turn it off yet," Cathal said. "Are you packed?"

"I am ready to go home. Are you?"

"Stop frowning at me. Your concern is going to give me gray hair."

Darragh snorted. "If either of us is going to get gray hair, it will be me because of *you*."

"Very funny. I will have you know I have been rather together as of late—"

"I know," Darragh said, suddenly serious. "You are going to make a great king. Ahren knew it, and I have always known it."

Cathal could feel his eyes watering, but per usual, he pushed it away. Darragh noticed though—as he noticed everything about Cathal—-and snickered.

"OK, OK, very funny. Let us not go and make the King of Teine cry."

"It would be an honor, sire. Your angelic tears gracing my bastard presence—"

Cathal held up a hand instinctively to silence him. "In my kingdom, you are no longer a bastard, merely my brother."

Without warning, Darragh grabbed Cathal in a fierce embrace.

And Cathal could have sworn Darragh shed a tear.

"You are too soft, my brother, for it makes me less hard and princely—"

Darragh hit the side of his shoulder, his laugh rumbling against his brother as they embraced. "We will figure this out, brother."

This.

The marriage contract.

The fact that they were about to leave to embark back home.

The necklace.

Everything. Shambles. Everything.

Cathal could feel the weight of it all beginning to take effect, for it was nearly as difficult to sort through all he knew without his breath stuttering. The world was not meant to carry this much darkness, this much hatred.

The creatures of the Isle were awakening in brutality. That much was certain.

And when they left the castle today, Cathal did not know if the world would look different than it did a few weeks prior when they left Teine to journey here.

Their quest was about to begin, though Cathal had known it was already well underway.

"Do you fear the wraiths?" Darragh asked, pulling apart from Cathal.

"I fear all which may have also awoken. Do you remember the teachings from the school Maesters? As children?"

"The tales we studied about different parts of the Isle?" Darragh asked, though he clearly knew what Cathal was referring to.

Cathal wondered for a moment if Orlaith knew the scope, given that she had never really ventured from these walls of her castle. She had no parent to give her details, though she surely had to read about the creatures of the Isle in her books from the library.

Right?

"There is much to be concerned about if it is true . . ." Cathal started as the door to the chambers swung open.

Orlaith stood before them, her cheeks slightly flushed and her gaze alight.

Cathal wished in this moment that she did not look so joyous. If only she knew what he wore around his neck.

Just and Mercy help them all.

"Are you just about ready?" Orlaith asked, looking between them.

Not knowing who "you" referenced, they both replied, "Yes."

She nodded and opened the door with her left arm as she gestured outside the door. "Then off to Teine we go."

And so, they followed, though Cathal paused at the doorway. Looking back at the chambers of the castle of Criostal, he breathed in and out and wished that all he feared were mere falsities.

And off they went.

CHAPTER 32

ORLAITH

The road was less dark than Orlaith imagined it to be.

As a child she dreamt of winding roads of darkness, clouds rolling in darker than the soot at the pit of a fire, and winds so torrential that it could be none other than the Gods themselves who could bring Teine to its knees. However, that was not what the road was in actuality.

It was her kingdom, she realized. The border, as it began to approach, was no more than some metaphorical line that guided them.

She had a lot of time to think on this carriage ride, the boys across from her not saying much of anything. Close quarters, as it would seem, were positively awkward with the royalty of Teine when they had nothing to talk about.

The Maesters gave her a carriage to take as if she were some doll. She knew it was safer—more discrete. Especially since she was traveling with the King of Teine.

But still, it drove her mad to be at the precipice of freedom and not be able to taste it.

Instead, she merely tasted Cathal's sarcasm and Darragh's impending stares.

"Why in the name of the two kingdoms is this carriage so bloody hot?" Orlaith dabbed the front of her forehead with a silk towelette. She was feeling as though dramatics would be necessary to endure being cooped up with these two, especially since it was either talk to them or keep *thinking*.

"You complain so much for a queen; it is rather sickening to my soul," Cathal practically moaned in reply, clearly affected by the heat, but refusing to admit defeat in the face of Orlaith. "If you projectile, I do hope it is outside."

"I'll make sure to aim for your face—"

"CATHAL!" Darragh roared, his face beet red from the impropriety of his flesh and blood. "Orlaith, would you like us to stop?"

"Do not call me Orlaith. I'm not your casual acquaintance."

Rolling his eyes, he growled, "Queen of Criostal, Oh Beautiful One, and Overlord of the Emerald Crown, would you like me to open the fucking window?"

"You are funny, Darragh. You know that, right?" Cathal chided, sitting up as though he were completely refreshed.

"You are the least funny person I have ever met, Darragh," Orlaith spat at him, leaning against the back of the carriage dramatically. "And this is the hottest I have ever been."

"I beg to differ. I seem to recall that women tend to look better with their clothes—"

"CATHAL!" Darragh shouted, his voice filled now with distaste.

This was what Cathal did. He pushed and pushed until the line was crossed between having a good time and being a menace. He was beyond the boundary now, but something about the Queen of Criostal had him completely out of control. She brought it out of him, the uncontrollable.

She hid a smile as she pretended to dab her upper lip with the handkerchief, enjoying how riled up he was. Maybe this was not so bad after all. Maybe being alone with her thoughts was worse than talking to them . . .

"Does Cathal's tendency to be so indecent bother you, Darragh?" she asked nonchalantly, refusing to make eye contact with him as she continued to push and push and push. It would be fun to see how long she could go before he exploded.

"Yes," Darragh said. "It is a lot of work to bring him back down to baseline once he gets out of control."

"Baseline?" Cathal said in the huff of a laugh. "You do not know the first thing, Darragh, about being on any base—"

"CATHAL!" they both shouted simultaneously.

Darragh's face went beet red.

Orlaith smirked.

She won.

Checkmate.

"You know, these woods are quite famous in the lands of Teine," Cathal chided to both of them casually, gazing out the window in wonder. "There are said to be wolven in your kingdom."

Orlaith rolled her eyes. "Childhood tales."

Darragh raised an eyebrow, but of course Cathal was the one to continue. "You have never seen one?"

"No. I have not." Now she was unsure of herself.

"Oh, come on, your Majesty. You will not even entertain the idea of anything other than a human or an elf on the Isle?"

"I have never heard of a wolf in my lands, your Majesty." But there it was, the faint touch of grief as it swept into her mind. Dealla, in her last time with Orlaith, had told her as much. She really knew nothing of her kingdom. For all she knew, they could be real.

And that was terrifying within itself.

How could she be expected to take the crown when she did not know what existed on her own Isle?

"I was told childhood tales of them with their long claws, their sharp fangs, and their territorial nature,"

"Cathal . . ." Darragh warned.

As Orlaith gazed up, she saw he was looking at her. Really looking at her. He must have seen the change in her disposition. That pain overtaking her once more.

"To be frank," Orlaith said, not sure why in the name of the Gods she was sharing anything with this loon. "My times out of the castle are . . . few and far between."

If it was even possible, Darragh raised an eyebrow higher.

And if it was even more possible, Cathal was silent.

She guessed she had the floor then. Nervously, she tapped her fingers on the hilt of Oidhe, which sat next to the door of the carriage.

"It was Dealla who encouraged me on more than one

occasion to step out of the castle," she gulped, their silence as deafening as it was concerning. "That first night that we all ran into one another in Haversin . . ."

"Do not tell me that was your first night out?" Cathal questioned, horrified.

Despite her efforts to remain neutral, she laughed. "No, not my first night. But my first in quite a while."

"Why?" Darragh asked, before turning that dark red color again.

Why was he so embarrassed when talking to her?

"Being crowned on your sixth day of life does not have many perks."

"I cannot imagine it would," Cathal replied seriously, a frown encroaching on his dark eyebrows.

A beat of silence passed before Darragh opened his mouth to say something, and then suddenly, the carriage shook.

Instinctively, Orlaith reached for Oidhe, but it was Darragh who was already holding his short sword. *How had he managed to grab it that fast?*

With a long finger pressed to his lips, he motioned for them to remain quiet. Reaching for the door to the carriage, he inhaled a sharp breath and threw it open with a grunt.

Orlaith screamed.

Dealla's face flashed before her mind.

Terror ripped through her once more, and she was not certain her heart was still beating.

They were surrounded by dogs.

CHAPTER 33

DARRAGH

They had tried to tell Orlaith—mere moments ago —but she had remained steadfast. Cathal had even mentioned to him before he left that he had hinted at the terrors of the world. The real world beyond the castle walls. But by the time they realized she was not uncertain— no—she had no idea of the reality that existed beyond the walls of her world. She was so fucking stubborn . . .

Yet the queen was the first one out of the carriage.

And Darragh could not help but have his mouth hang open.

She was magnificent.

And suddenly, he found himself afraid for the wolven as much as he feared for her.

And then he blinked in a flash, realizing she was the wolf.

And then he had nothing more to be afraid of.

CHAPTER 34

ORLAITH

Elves were fast.

Orlaith was faster.

Catapulting herself from the carriage, she began her dance.

Weaving through the intruders with Oidhe held high, she commanded their attention. The wolves' big dark eyes all followed her in unison as she moved among the flowers of the field without a whisper of a sound. Ever so faintly, the sound of talons scraping themselves through the dried dirt on the ground could be heard for her. As they came into clearer vision and out of the brush, their different colors of fur blurred in her vision with her speed as she did anything she could to try to move them away.

Until merely moments before, she did not think these creatures existed.

And now here she stood, her turquoise eyes wide and filled with them in her vision.

And now here she stood, a pain in her heart about her best friend who was taken from her by darkness reincarnate.

She could *feel* Cathal and Darragh behind her, their weapons unsheathed and their breathing ragged. And she swore she could *feel* Dealla too.

"Stand your ground," she said, still holding her sword high as she stopped. "We do not want anyone getting hurt here."

Arranged in a triangle, the dark-colored dogs stepped back as a gray one came forward. Fangs snarled in retaliation to her elven tongue, and it took everything within her not to shirk backward. But for being a woman who trained with a sword as a release, she knew she was ready for combat, all lack of experiences aside.

"That might be easier said than done," Cathal's voice rang warily from behind her.

"Orlaith," Darragh's voice behind her strained painfully. It was almost enough to get her to turn around, his voice this unhinged. She had never heard him sound like that before, not at the death of his grandfather, not at the sound of *anything*.

The gray wolf stepped forward in his entirety, teeth barred, and eyes filled with rage. Though it was not the physicality of the beast that shocked her, more so the deep voice that filled her mind, *"Heir to the Emerald Crown, what brings you to my lands?"*

Orlaith did not look behind her to see if Cathal and Darragh's minds were also infiltrated. By the way they still stood, she assumed she alone was the one to bear this message.

"I am traveling to the crown," she stammered, hating herself a little more for being afraid.

"*You are not welcome, for it is you that brought this harsh destiny upon these lands.*" The wolf gestured around to the few that stood around him. "*I promised your father I would never harm you as long as you stayed away from my lands, and now that you are here, I must fulfill my promise to him. They were gifted to me and my family, and I forbid the rot that has begun to overtake Teine to come to me and my family.*"

Shock bristled through Orlaith, shooting down her spine and causing her hands to grip Oidhe so tightly that her knuckles were turning white. And before she had the chance to respond, to beg, to ask questions—he struck.

"ORLAITH!" Darragh's voice pierced her like the breath of a first winter as the wolven descended.

She could barely hear him over the growl of the gray wolf that she danced around, refusing to land a blow, but trying to usher him from her at every step she took.

Out of her peripheral, she could see Cathal doing the same, holding his dagger at an arm's length and jumping over any that tried to strike at him. He was marvelous.

She could not bring herself to look at Darragh, though she could feel him getting closer to her. He was descending and moving with stealth as well, but it was clear that Orlaith and Cathal were the targets.

What in the name of the Gods had her father done to get her barred from these lands?

Opening her mouth to try to reason with the wolven, she was cut off as the creature lunged—but not for her.

"DARRAGH!" she screamed before she had a chance to think.

And then she was running.

The gray wolf had pinned him to the ground, drawing her out of the thrush. But she had lost so many people already, and she would not lose another. Even one that she was not sure how she felt about in this moment. The only thing that lived within her: fear.

Light as a feather on her feet, she tore through the flowers of the field and stuck out her sword toward the beast. Grimacing, she turned her head to the side and braced herself. She did not want to take a life. She had never taken the life of anything. It was not the way of the elves.

In a flash, she felt Oidhe enter the leg of the wolf which had pinned Darragh. It howled— cruel, broken, and in shock. Venom pulsated from its teeth, white thick foam that made the animal turn from beautifully impressive to dangerously haunting.

Lifting her gaze to level with the creature, she could see the anger which blitzed through the amber streaked gold of its eyes. She would not show fear, despite the shaking that wrecked her hands as she ripped the sword from the wolf's side. And in that moment, she felt sorry for something she could not explain. Whatever her father had done, whatever deal had been struck she had broken unintentionally. She felt it something sacred, a bond as ancient as these creatures.

"*You will pay for this,*" the wolf hissed in her ears. "*Consider this a parting gift.*"

And suddenly, she did not fear them, for she felt like she

deserved whatever consequence befell her at the expense of her father.

Whatever atonement she was paying for, she would welcome it with open arms.

With a snarl, the wolf lunged toward her free hand with a snap. Teeth collided with her elven skin, and she was immediately overtaken with the venom of the wolves' hatred for her. She could see it in her gaze, overtaken with images of her father in this very field with the wolf she had just stabbed.

He was begging, as far as she could tell, and the wolf was hungry for vengeance. She felt that disappointment, one thing she knew all too well. It clawed at her, begging to take her down. Maybe it was the fault of her legacy that the Isle was in the state it was in.

As she made a step forward—whether it was to beg the wolf for forgiveness or cry out for a helping hand was unclear —the wolf took off, limping with a howl as the others followed in his stead.

Knees collapsing into the field below her, she could only hear one word being screamed through the air intermixed with her own name. A word she had not heard in many years, but one that was a part of her studies. It was territorial, one that she could not place, but it awoke something in her. It snapped into place.

And the word lingered, even as she closed her eyes to nothingness.

Anam.

CHAPTER 35

CATHAL

The wind ripped past Cathal's face so fiercely that he was not sure if it was how fast they were running or the power which lived in Darragh's veins.

Cathal had never seen Darragh so destroyed.

So unkempt.

So *unlike* himself.

Darragh had rushed over to Orlaith when she saved him with lighting speed, so light on his feet for just being chastised by a wolf twice the size of himself. Holding her upright by her arms, Darragh then demanded that they ride to Haversin on bareback. It would be the fastest way.

Cathal unlatched the horses in the carriage with Oidhe—praying to the Gods that Orlaith would forgive him for touching her sword if she ever were to find out—and helped Darragh get her on the horse with him.

Cathal could not put his finger on it, but he knew by the way Darragh was holding her not to suggest to him that he take her. He was the faster rider—always had been—but the look of dismay across his brother's face confirmed he would not allow Cathal to touch her right now. It was peculiar, but they had not a moment to spare.

Cathal trailed them as Darragh rode like the bloody wind.

~

As soon as they made their way from the tree line—leaving the forest, the fields, and roads behind them—Haversin appeared.

The buildings they saw weeks ago had a different appeal to them now, for before they were all promise of a new kingdom and a party to meet a queen. Now they represented all that had happened since then: a true crossroads between who they were before they journeyed to Criostal and who they were now.

Darragh did not relent, even as the townspeople came into view, and the streets became crowded with pedestrians.

"Dar!" Cathal yelped, trying to weave through the people while keeping pace. "Dar! Slow down!"

"WE NEED A HEALER!" He was yelling, his face riddled with concern and his voice cracking.

What in the name of the Gods was happening?

"Darragh! Slow down—"

Almost on cue, Cathal spotted what Darragh had been rushing toward. A big black iron sign hung above a large white door, with the words *APOTHECARY* ordaining the front.

"In the name of Just and Mercy—" Cathal said as Darragh jumped off his horse.

"GRAB HER, CAW! HELP ME!"

Now Cathal was truly terrified. He never spoke like this, not to him, and surely not to anyone.

In one swift motion, he unmounted his horse, tied their reins together, and found himself carrying the Queen of Criostal by the feet while Darragh grabbed her under her arms.

Her head lulled to the right as Darragh shoved open the door with his back, and for the first time since the queen had fallen over, Cathal was truly scared. Had she been unconscious this whole time? How did Darragh know something was so amiss? The wolf had bitten her. He had seen it. But had something else happened for her to still be rendered unconscious?

"HELP!" Darragh was yelling with effort as they dragged Orlaith to the counter of the apothecary.

Cathal tried to gather some awareness of his surroundings. Potions lined nearly every part of the dark wooden walls. Shelves stacked to the brim with magical potions, bottles, and a multitude of flowers which were unrecognizable to him. What he could feel was the power within the walls radiating off the shelves, clearly a place of extreme practice and prose. He was certain this place, whatever it was, harbored great power and knowledge.

He prayed to the Gods that this place would be enough to save the Queen of Criostal from whatever had affected her after her run-in with the wolven.

As they set her down gently, Darragh grabbed her arm and felt for a pulse.

"Is she . . . dead?" Cathal asked, fearing the worst given Darragh's reaction.

"No!" Darragh growled. "But she is close."

"Let me help her," a voice sounded from the back of the apothecary.

Rushing forward, an elf seemingly comparable in age stepped forward. Her black hair cascaded down her arms which were covered in the dust of flowers and potions. Her hands nearly glowed green from the pollen, and the dark green sleeves of her simple gown soaked with whatever she had been working on in the back of the shop.

"What happened?" she asked, her blue eyes piercing into Cathal's.

But it was Darragh who spoke. "Wolven. She was bitten on her hand, the venom spreading—"

Cathal froze. How in the name of the Gods did Darragh know more about wolven then than him?

"Just and Mercy," the elf huffed, terror creeping into her voice. "Wolven? Attacking? That is not normal—"

"I do not give a fuck if it is not normal. It *happened*, and she needs help or she is going to—"

With a snarl, the black-haired elf pointed to the shelf closest to Darragh. "Shut up, and hand me the black potion behind you."

When Darragh froze at her jarring tone, she shouted again, "NOW!"

Frozen as if paralyzed from fear alone, Cathal grunted

and ran over to the wall. The potion was easy to spot, black and glittering in a bottle shaped like a skull.

How endearing.

"Here," Cathal said, handing it to her with shaking hands.

Uncapping it with her teeth, the elf dumped half of the potion on her hands and immediately began rubbing it into Orlaith's bite wound on her hand. With her other hand, she handed it to Darragh, "Make yourself useful, or get out of my shop. I cannot have you in here worrying. I need *help*."

Silently, Darragh took the bottle.

"Good," she said. "You." She gestured to Cathal. "Hold her head upright. She is going to be hot to the touch—just ignore it for now. Her fever is quite high from the poison. The tonic will take it down, but she *has* to drink."

"You." She nodded toward Darragh, who seemed to have resumed some of his natural color. "Pour it down her throat. She is going to gag—it is fine, but she must get it into her system."

Darragh opened his mouth—whether to breathe or ask a question Cathal was equally unsure—when the black-haired elf yelled, "NOW!"

As Cathal's hands made contact with the temples of Orlaith's head, he nearly jerked them back. Had she been this hot while Darragh and her were riding? No wonder he was so bloody concerned.

Darragh poured the black glittering liquid down her throat, his eyes still heavily latent with worry, when Orlaith grunted. The world seemed to sag as they heard Orlaith cough, the color resuming into her cheeks nearly instantly.

"Orlaith?" Darragh asked, his voice shaking with fear and hope at the same time.

She made no sound, yet it was clear she was no longer inches from death.

"Thank you," Darragh half-sobbed toward the black-haired elf.

She smiled, her blue eyes rimmed with tears. Had she been crying?

"Thank you very much," Cathal reiterated, feeling quite overcome himself.

"It is the job," she said, looking down at Orlaith and rubbing her hands on the front of her dress modestly. "Please, take her upstairs gently. You can rest here for the evening. There are two beds upstairs. She can take one, and if you both do not mind sharing the other to look after her—"

"It is no worry," Cathal said after a pause. Clearly, Darragh was spent.

"Do you need any food? Tea?" the elf asked earnestly, her face much kinder than it had been when she blitzed Darragh as she saved Orlaith's life.

Darragh put his hands over his eyes and yawned, answering the silent question that Cathal was practically tele-pathically asking him.

"Not tonight, but thank you for your generosity. We are feeling—quite tired from the trials and tribulations of the day, if you can imagine."

The elf smiled at Cathal, then looked back at Orlaith and Darragh with some concern furrowing her brow.

"I can imagine," she said softly, her face remaining unreadable.

"May I get your name?" he asked, as he started to grab Orlaith by the shoulder to carry her upper body upstairs.

"Eithne," she replied. "My name is Eithne."

AFTER BRINGING ORLAITH UPSTAIRS, insisting to Eithne that they would not require anything more than a wash bin for the evening, and laying down in the bed, Cathal could not stop himself from uttering the next four words. "Darragh, what was that?"

"I have never been that terrified before, Caw," Darragh whispered, looking very far away at nothing.

"We have not known her for very long, you know. She could be a mass murderer."

"I am being serious, brother." Darragh replied. "I feel as though she is the type to show her true colors early."

Cathal could swear he could see the corners of his brother's mouth twitching upward, despite the exhaustion he exuded.

At this point, he was truly concerned.

"Right you are. She wears her emotions on her sleeve, does she not?" He paused, feeling dramatically poetic. "Fear, anger, sadness . . . you see them on her before I think she even recognizes they live within her."

"Fearlessness."

"What?" Cathal asked, not understanding Darragh's interjection.

"That is what I saw on her today when the wolven

appeared. She did not hesitate for a moment before she had her sword in hand."

Cathal almost snorted. Darragh was too observant. "It seems she has made an admirer of you."

It was dark in the room, but Cathal could have sworn Darragh flushed dark red in the candlelight. His hair was illuminated in this light, a similar hue to it, so it would be impossible to tell.

"I am going to tell you something, Cathal," Darragh whispered. "And I need you to never repeat it. I fear what would happen if it were to get in the wrong hands, and I fear for the fate of the three of us when I utter the word I screamed when she was bitten."

"What?" Cathal said, cocking his head to the side as he lay on the pillow horizontal to his brother. "What could you have possibly said that would bring the world to its knees like you are suggesting? And how could you possibly have known that wolven bites were so dangerous? Is that why you lost your mind when she went down? You could have told me. Clearly, I do not listen enough during schooling—"

Darragh took a deep breath, his scar looking so harsh in this low candlelight against his tanned skin, and ignoring all inquiries that Cathal had made when he whispered too lowly that his voice could have passed for a breeze in the wind.

"Anam."

And then Cathal swore, the necklace on his neck suddenly weighing what he imagined it would feel like to hold up the whole Isle.

CHAPTER 36

ORLAITH

Darkness circled in the Queen of Criostal's mind, crackling and whispering words of hatred. Twisting, she fought hard against them, reaching for her light.

But *something* was blocking, a wall of dark matter much like the smoke that she had seen before King Ahren was stabbed.

Dealla hated you when she died.

Your father started this war.

The wraiths are coming for you.

The wolven hate you.

You deserve to die.

"No," Orlaith hissed. Whether it was in her mind or audible, she could not tell. She did not care. "It is not true."

Light would not relent against the stream of endless evil that pounded within her. She could sense it in her bones, her blood coated with the same eeriness that had crept into her castle.

"Of course, it is true, Orlaith Kearan, Queen of the Light. You may have power, you may have a crown, but everything you have ever had has been nothing but a thread of what the world could promise you. Join us, Orlaith Kearan, join us and rule as you were born to rule. Join us, like your father could not. Accept your defeat, and accept power on our altar of darkness."

Breathing unevenly, Orlaith dug deeply into her mind. It was no different from pushing through a solo training session, memorizing politics prior to a meeting with adversary maesters, or even sparring with Cathal's tongue.

This was her training.

This was who she was born to be.

A fucking queen.

"Darkness has nothing on light that shines."

She knew who this was, despite the lack of cognition within her. She could feel him, that shadowy presence that had come to her castle and taken the lives of other elves.

With a smile, she envisioned herself looking at the Wraith King and smiling. To show him that she was truly not afraid.

And he should be.

And then she dove deeper into herself than she had ever let herself explore before and erupted with starlight.

SHE WOKE UP SCREAMING, two hands on her, frantically touching her jawline. She was not sure what they were searching for, but she heard a door click.

Did someone leave? But the hands were still touching her?

And then she heard the voice, filled with the starlight she had felt in her bones in her dream. *It was a dream, was it not?*

"Anam," the voice was whispering.

The word seemed to grace her lips like she imagined the whisper of a kiss would, in a tongue far more powerful than her own language. It was not an elven term, that was for sure, but an ancient one. It sat on the tip of her tongue—the word—but for whatever reason she could not formulate the ability to speak it from her own lips. It was as if the word was not ready, the language and meaning so deeply powerful that whatever test she was going to have to pass to be allowed to do such a thing was currently null and void.

"Anam," it whispered again, hopeful and desperately broken all at once.

She had never heard anyone speak like that before, let alone about herself.

She groaned in response—chills running through her blood at the soul of the word—unable to even open her eyes to greet the face of the one who spoke. Exhaustion weighed heavy on her eyelids, her head lulling back and forth as though she were no more than an infant.

Trying to grasp onto some sort of reality, she let her mind wander as the voice continued to serenade her with a word that sounded so much like her own name should. Except she knew it was not. But it was all the same, so familiar and so *right*.

After a moment of reaching—she caught onto something—a tether against all of the darkness that swam within her.

A flash of red.

The howl of wolven.

The blood of an elven queen.

The shadows of the Wraith King.

She gasped, looking back and realizing what she had done.

"Shh," the voice said, helping her lay down once more on what she believed was a bed. "Sleep, my Queen. Sleep."

Commanding.

Yet, that same familiarity that Orlaith could not place.

"Sleep, Anam."

CHAPTER 37

CATHAL

Cathal had slipped out of the room the moment Orlaith started to scream. He could feel that his presence was wildly unwanted, and frankly, after seeing Darragh the way he had been earlier, he knew his brother had whatever it was that was to come with her under control.

Additionally, it did not feel right of him to sit there and comfort her, when he knew the emerald chain around his neck called to him more and more to kill her. And now that they were on their way to get the crown? The doom was impending.

Darragh had dashed to her side in an instant, lighter on his feet than he had been in days. He had to have been exhausted. They were elves, but they were not impervious to human characteristics. He still needed to sleep and eat.

A flash of black hair entered his peripheral vision, and he found himself turning off all of his current fears. This elf saved Orlaith, and she deserved his full attention. Who would he spar with if Orlaith was gone? The thought suddenly had his chest feeling concave.

Did he . . . *like* the Queen of Criostal? Not like, like *that*. But over the last few weeks since their baptism by fire in the tavern, he had grown weirdly fond of the queen. She was difficult, but she had so many qualities to be admired.

And he could not shake the image of her stabbing a wolf to save his brother from harm. He could never—would never, forget such a thing.

She saved Darragh, therefore—by association—she had saved him. For Darragh was his soul. The parts of him that made him truly special, no crown necessary.

He owed the Queen of Criostal everything. And he would tell her himself as soon as she woke up. Orlaith Kearan was a lot of things, but she was definitely too stubborn to die.

"How is your brother—he is your brother, correct?" Eithne asked, her blue eyes shadowed by worry.

"Familial resemblance?" Cathal asked, rather surprised she had guessed. They were not exactly the look and sound of brothers.

"It is the eyes; they are both haunted by the same darkness."

Raising an eyebrow, Cathal decided to shift directions. He had enough talk of being haunted these last few weeks to reminisce with a total stranger. "She woke up yelling, seems as though she will be fine."

Crossing her arms over her chest, Eithne seemed to catch Cathal's gist. "She is lucky your brother rushed her here. Just a few more minutes, and the poison could have killed her."

"Get many patients with wolven bites?"

Eithne paused, pondering. Did she not want to tell him something? "Wolven bites are extremely rare, for they are creatures of old."

"I was schooled," Cathal said, feeling annoyed she assumed he knew absolutely nothing about anything. Even though the reality was that Darragh knew the weight of what a wolven bite truly meant, and he had no idea. Maybe he should pay closer attention to details . . .

"Then let me refresh you. Wolven bites are incredibly dangerous—as they are rare—because wolven are relatively peaceful creatures. They tend to keep to their territories, keeping the peace between all living things they encounter."

"That? You call what we went through peace?" Cathal nearly snorted, the growls still ringing in his ears.

He had never seen such aggression so instantly. It was like they had come to a halt, and then once Orlaith stepped out of the carriage, chaos had ensued. It became a war very quickly. And if Cathal knew anything, he knew that to be at war it had to escalate. It did not just happen.

"Except," she said, lifting a long ethereal hand, "when they encounter someone who has a wolven curse on them."

"What in the name of the Gods is a wolven curse?"

"When a wolf has been wronged or double-crossed, they make a vow. Normally, this vow is the agreement or concession between both members of the vow, and if the vow is broken, the curse ensues."

She paused, as if waiting for Cathal to speak again, but he said nothing. Orlaith had a wolven curse upon her? How could this—

"I am guessing she did not know."

"There is a lot the three of us do not know, it seems," Cathal whispered, running a hand through his black hair in exasperation. "A curse. Will she know now?"

"It is a gift that she lived without knowing, but the curse itself will be at the forefront now that a wolf actually bit her." Eithne took a deep breath. "You do not have to tell me if you do not wish to—who you are and what your name is, or why in the name of the Gods she would have been attacked by a wolf…"

Good, because I am not telling you.

"But just know that these are dangerous times, and to be wary always. I am not sure how long you wanted to stay—"

"Not long," Cathal interjected as she continued. "We will wait until she is better, and then we shall leave."

Apprehensively, Eithne ignored his comment. "But the King of Teine was murdered at the queen's castle not long before you arrived. If Teine is without a king—"

"Prince Cathal lives," Cathal dared to say, keeping his expression neutral. There was a part of him that wanted to tell her who he was, yet there was another part that demanded to keep his identity a secret.

Why should he trust her?

"Even so, it is the unrest that follows the death of a monarch that terrifies me so." Her eyes raked him from head to toe. "I do not know how old you are, or if you are too young to remember when the King and Queen of Criostal died, but—"

"How old are you?" Cathal asked, unable to keep the surprise out of his voice. He had assumed by the look of her that she was about his age.

"Older than you, I take it," she said with a smirk, her dark blue eyes shimmering with mystery. With a long finger, she ran it down the front of his black tunic. "Do you not know not to ask an elf how old they are?"

"Do you not know not to touch people you do not know?" he drawled lazily, batting his eyelashes as he normally did.

Leaning so close to him that he could feel her hot breath on his cheek, she whispered, "Something tells me that you do not mind."

"Interesting assumption for someone you just met."

"I cannot explain it," she whispered, taking a step backward and tying her hands behind her back. "But it is as if I already know you. You are so easy—"

"What a choice of words," he said softly with a laugh bubbling within him.

"Not what I meant!" she said, her hand covering her mouth as she laughed. "I merely mean you have a way about you. It is refreshing to see. You are . . . so alive. More people could be more like you in that way."

"In what way do you mean?" he asked, though he knew exactly what she was trying to say.

Everyone had always said that about him. He was just that.

Easy.

Easy to talk to.

Easy to be around.

He was royal through and through, after all.

But he knew in his heart that he was the opposite.

Difficult.

He was difficult.

He guessed that was a part of being a royal.

Maybe.

"When you talk, colors are brighter. The winds are at ease as you stand here in front of me—"

"Quite a heavy word choice for someone who you do not know."

She flushed, continuing to back up toward the door that he assumed led to her own bedroom. "I might not need to know your name, but it would be easier to speak to you in the morning that way after you get a good night's rest."

"Cormac," he said without flinching, thinking back to the young elf he had met in the capital city a few weeks prior. "My name is Cormac. Familial name not important."

"Well, Cormac," she said, turning toward her door. "Sleep tight."

CHAPTER 38

ORLAITH

The stars were dying.

Flowers were wilting.

Gems no longer sparkling.

Or maybe it was her that was dying. It would not be the first time in the recent history of the Isle that a monarch had died.

Groaning, Orlaith rolled over. The sun was perched directly in front of her window, the heat so unbearable she was sure the Gods were trying to melt her.

Maybe she should let them.

She could hear stirring behind her, though she could not bring herself to turn around. Despite being unconscious, she knew who she was sharing a room with. Where she was, she could not pinpoint. It would require opening her eyes, which she was not ready for yet. Just another moment of rest—

Clang!

What could only be the incessant noise of a steel water jug hit the floor with the most obnoxious clamor.

Well, that got her to turn around.

With a hiss, she flipped in her bed and met the concerned gaze of Darragh. Surprise hit her straight in the chest, for she was sure this type of annoyance could only be associated with Cathal's presence.

"Orlaith?" he asked, hesitantly.

There was a question lingering on his lips beyond her name—Orlaith knew it—but found she could not ask anything herself. She was tongue-tied, stuck, and utterly confused why for the first time in her life she genuinely had nothing to say other than . . .

"Thank you." She repositioned her legs, so she did not look so awkward in the bed.

"For what?" he asked, his voice softer than a gust of wind.

She noticed in this moment how shadowed his under eyes were. His red hair appeared less bright too, more amber than its usual fire. He was haunted by something.

"For saving me," she said with a groan, hating to admit it. "I do not remember much—"

"What do you remember?"

She closed her eyes, thinking hard about what she did in fact remember. There were so many wolven, and she had turned around . . .

"The wolf that threatened me was on top of you, and I—"

"I guess I am the one who should be thanking *you*," he said with a soft smile.

She realized he was wearing something different from when she last saw him. His tunic was a dark green, strings loose at the top that he did not bother to tie.

"Did you feel it?" she asked, her memory coming in waves.

"Feel what?" he asked, sitting down on the other bed slowly with caution.

She could hear his heart racing. It sounded almost human, the way it thundered within his chest. Was he nervous?

"I am not sure," she said with a huff. "I do not remember much after diving toward you."

"It was rather anti-climactic," a voice chided from the doorway.

Orlaith lifted her gaze to meet the smiling gaze of Cathal, his dark eyes dancing with amusement that she could not place.

"You stabbed that nasty wolf, the nasty wolf bit you, they ran away, and Darragh rode like the bloody devil to get you here."

"Ta-da," Darragh said sarcastically, lifting his arms bashfully.

"And where is here?" she asked, trying to muster the energy to sit up. She could tell that Darragh and Cathal lurched as she tried to do so, but she waved them off. She could do this. It was just a wolf bite—

"Haversin. The apothecary. Turns out wolf bites are *very* nasty. The owner here nearly had to cut off your arm to save you, but I said you liked your arm very much, and so you can thank me too." Cathal looked serious as he crossed his arms over his chest.

She noticed now too that he had changed as well. His dark blue tunic complemented him well, making him look like the true King of Teine. Or at least, more like he had looked at the castle when she first met him. Minus the mask.

Breathing heavy from the effort to sit up straight, Orlaith looked down at her hand which still stung and ignored his comments regarding the apothecary owner. Clearly, her arm remained.

And by the way Darragh was bristling at Cathal, she confirmed it was a mere fabrication.

There was a row of teeth marks, though they were sealed up with scars where she had been punctured. But what concerned her was the gray skin that coated her entire hand, as if the poison had started to desecrate her like a dead body. She lifted it, and out of the corner of her eye, she caught Darragh's horrified and ashamed gaze.

"This is new."

"A slight effect of the bite and the poison being contained." Cathal was blunt as Darragh remained silent. "A curse, some might say."

"Lovely," she said with all the sarcasm her exhausted body could muster. "So, all of the stories are true then? About the world?"

Darragh chuckled, though there was a darkness behind the sound that was wordlessly communicating he thought Orlaith was positively stupid. Or at least that was how she was interpreting it. "It would appear most are, my Queen."

"I am not your queen, and you know it," Orlaith said with a huffed laugh.

Within the blink of an eye, Darragh was a mere inch from her face. His eyes flashed with an emotion so intense Orlaith could have sworn she made it up. His scar, in this lighting, looking more like a part of him than ever. She was not afraid of him, yet her heart would not stop pounding as if she were.

"You are more my queen than you will ever know, Orlaith."

She nearly gasped, his gaze so intense and that feeling of déjà vu returning instantaneously. She knew he was telling her something, something she could not remember. His eyes gave everything away.

She would ask him about what he was not saying later, when they were alone. She could not seem to do anything seriously when she was with Cathal.

"Come, brother," Cathal's voice boomed from behind them.

Darragh blinked, as if coming back to himself, and backed away slowly. "Go back to sleep, Orlaith. We have all the time before we leave."

Lowering herself, she let herself do the one thing she never did—relax.

By the time the door clicked behind her, she was asleep once more.

CHAPTER 39

DARRAGH

Darragh knew Cathal was following him, despite his footsteps being silent.

And when the door shut, he was yelling.

"Bloody hell, Caw. What are we going to do? The closer we get her to the crown, the more we are testing the fates here—"

"We do not even know if Ahren's little curse in this bloody necklace is still valid . . ."

"Try to take off the necklace," Darragh demanded, his voice raising above his normal octave. He interlaced his hands behind his back, as if he were trying to prevent himself from ripping it off of Cathal's neck directly. "Try to take it off, Caw."

Cathal raised his arms to the clasp around the back and found that when his hands touched the golden chain, it was unbearably hot to the touch. "Gods! Bloody Grandfather . . ."

Darragh sunk to the ground, his hands in his red hair in dismay. "We cannot take her there, Cathal. We cannot do this."

Cathal sunk to his level, his stare all intention. "I will not lose you. You know what Grandfather said. If I do not—"

It made him sick. Orlaith was his godsdamned friend, but Darragh was his blood. His *brother*. He could not and would not lose him. He would not survive it.

"Cathal," Darragh's voice sounded. "I cannot lose her."

Anam.

It was an old elven term, one from the early days of the Isle. It was rather unusual to find one. Some lore called for the term to mean that of mates, the other half of one's soul, though the bond did not have to be returned. But when it snapped into place, for whatever reason the Gods had decided, there was no turning back.

A part of Cathal's heart sank, for if Orlaith never connected with Darragh as her own anam, he would walk the world for the rest of his life haunted by all that she was.

"Fuck!" Cathal shouted, standing immediately and smacking his hands into his face in irritation. "Darragh—we could not stay at that castle. With the wraiths—what happened to Grandfather . . . Shit! What happened to her friend Dealla!"

"I know, I know . . . She wants to bring you home, Cathal. Arranged marriage aside. She wants to bring her friend home."

"She wants the crown," Cathal said. "If I do not help her get it—"

"This is a shit show."

"Completely and utterly." Cathal paused.

Darragh stood, walking so close to Cathal's face that Cathal was unsure if Darragh was going to kiss him or punch him. "Dar, whatever are you doing?"

"We have to tell her. Let her choose. Let us figure out a way to break this curse. Get that godsdamned necklace off of you."

"I do not know, Dar—" Cathal said softly, looking around to make sure she was not standing behind them or something. That would be just his luck. She was starting to trust them. He could tell from the way she had woken up and lit up at their faces greeting her. "I do not want to lose this alliance—"

"The longer we wait, the worse it will be."

"You are her anam," Cathal whispered. "You tell her."

"You are the one wearing the bloody necklace . . ."

"She will take it better from you, Dar. You know it." He stepped an inch closer, his canines flashing in dominance. He hated pulling his shit with Dar, demonstrating he was the more powerful of the two of them.

But if this was going to be a brawl about power, Cathal knew what cards he had to play.

"Fuck you, Cathal," Darragh spat, turning and walking toward the door of the apothecary.

"Darragh!" he half-shouted.

But as Darragh slammed the door, he was resigned.

He would come around.

He had to.

That was the only way she would survive this betrayal. Darragh had not seen the glimmer in her eye when she talked of fulfilling her legacy. If they wanted to save her, Cathal was going to need to bring in every reinforcement he could to convince her.

But in the back of his mind, Cathal knew.

There would be nothing to get between the heir and her crown.

Even death itself.

CHAPTER 40

ORLAITH

Orlaith awoke to whispers that seemed to carry through the walls of the apothecary.

She could not make anything out, yet she knew it was Darragh and Cathal. Whatever they had been discussing was serious, she could tell due to the absence of laughter. She wondered what they could possibly be discussing and hoped it was not a plan to recover the crown without her. They needed her.

Gasping with surprise, Orlaith noticed the world outside was completely dark. How long had she been out? Palming her right temple with the palm of her hand, she breathed in and out rhythmically. In waves, it started to come back to her. She had been awake earlier and had been talking to Darragh and Cathal.

"Where is my sword?" she whispered, sitting up quickly and feeling the blood rush to her head. Swinging her legs over abrasively, she stood. Vision blacking in and out, she breathed deeply again with her eyes closed.

"I will not break. I will not be weak. I am queen," she whispered over and over again. It was more than a mantra and a belief; it was the cure to her suffering. It was all that she had to hold on to or be forced to reckon with the madness within.

Weakness was unacceptable.

As the darkness passed, she stood again, her feet moving slowly toward the door. She looked down for the first time to notice she had been changed into a black shift, clearly a nightgown. Heat flooded to her cheeks at the thought. Who had put her in this gown? Darragh? Cathal? *Oh Gods...*

Pushing on the door, it creaked open slowly as she grabbed onto the banister. She knew she should probably be resting, since the wolf bite had obviously been extremely powerful if it had attacked her in such a way, but she needed her sword.

Nothing would get between her and her sword.

As she rounded the final step, she heard his voice before she raised her gaze to see him.

"You look like shit, your Majesty," Cathal said, leaning up against the wall of potions, looking at his nails nonchalantly.

Gods, she hated him. Sometimes.

Resigned, she whispered with exhaustion, her breath coming rapidly from her descent and being so weak. "And I feel it too, your Majesty."

Without warning, she began to slump against the wall, her shoulder colliding with a grunt.

In an instant, Cathal was at her side, all joking aside. "What are you doing out of bed, Orlaith? You should be resting."

"Stop mothering me," she managed to grunt out, feeling that exhaustion so strongly now. She leaned up against him heavily, her shoulder nearly putting all of her weight on his forearm.

"It is not every day a friend of mine gets bit by a wolf," he said softly.

Orlaith looked up at him and noticed his blue eyes seemed more haunted than they had last. She fought the urge to expend energy and ask him how he was doing, when she knew she had just enough strength to ask him where her sword was.

And then it hit her—he called her his friend.

"Where is Oidhe?"

Cathal's eyebrows raised, as if the question brought him back from wherever he was lost in. "Over here," he gestured, walking her toward the front table of the shop.

Lifting her by the hips, he set her down on the edge of the table and unwrapped the sword which had been covered in cloth. "Safe and sound, your Majesty."

Orlaith closed her eyes and smiled. "Were you the one to save Oidhe?"

"Yes, I managed to snag it from the ground when you were unconscious."

"Thank you," she breathed out. "Thank you for choosing my sword over me."

Cathal nearly choked. "It was more like Darragh had

you, and I knew you would kill me from the beyond if I lost your sword."

She chuckled, and then pondered for a second before asking, "Do you believe in a beyond?"

Opening her eyes, she noticed the under-eye circles on his own face, much like Darragh's. Were they always there, or did they get there in the last few days?

"I believe in it because if I did not, how do we keep going? Just and Mercy are the two Gods we praise in our culture, but you know as well as I that there are others. The Isle is not limited to just what *we* celebrate, you know."

She reached out her hand, tracing his jawline softly. "I think that is the only way anyone can survive this world."

"By what?" he asked, his left eyebrow quirked up in question.

"By believing in something we cannot see."

"What if there was a third God?" Cathal asked quietly, his amber eyes near black.

Orlaith pondered, considering all she knew in her life and how she had realized since the royalty of Teine had come into her life that she knew nothing.

"I guess it is possible," she whispered back. "But what would be the reasoning? Why have another God to rule besides Just and Mercy?"

"Because the world cannot thrive on Just and Mercy as conceptual Gods, Orlaith."

She blinked twice, unsure she was understanding.

"The Gods are in charge of all, supposedly, correct?" he pushed.

"Yes," she said, with an unexpected lack of firmness.

"Then where is the God of the punishments? Where is the God of Death? Are you telling me the world is based on Justification and Merciful action alone?"

"Cathal, where is this coming from?"

He took a step closer to her, intense yet soft in his amber gaze. "You need to stop being so godsdamned complacent, Orlaith, as do I. That wolf almost murdered you. You could have been attacked at your own castle when the wraiths came, and you do not even know who stands at your feet—"

"Do not tell me how to be a queen—" She kept her voice low, but felt that familiar return of the fire within her belly.

"Then bloody act like one," he growled. "Maybe then I will be inspired to do the same if I take my own throne."

If?

Opening his mouth to speak again, he suddenly looked desperate when the door chimed, and a woman stepped through the threshold. She was carrying a wicker basket filled with herbs and other remedies. Her black hair was the color of midnight itself, so much so that Orlaith looked down at her own hair to admire the contrast. As her gaze lifted to meet her own, she smiled softly with a look of surprise upon her full lips.

"Glad to see you are awake," she said, her voice calming and steady. "My name is Eithne."

"You are the one who saved me," Orlaith said, bowing her head.

"Yes," she said, looking at Cathal. "But it was Cormac and his brother who brought you here."

Orlaith paused, but she had played the part of different people so many times in her life that she did not miss more than a heartbeat before she said, "Yes, I would not be much of anything without Cormac and his brother."

Out of the corner of her eye, she saw Cathal gulp. She gave him a look that said, *You are a rat bastard,* before asking the question that erupted throughout her head without a warning or a rhyme or reason.

"Where is he?"

"He—"

"I saw him go into the tavern in town," Eithne said, moving toward the back of her store with her supplies. "He appeared . . . with the need to cool off."

"Gods," Cathal whispered. "I can go and get him."

"No," Orlaith nearly growled, weirdly acknowledging how possessive she was in this moment, but choosing not to dwell on it for a second longer. "We should get him together."

"Or—" he started. "I am not sure if you are well enough . . ."

"Fresh air will do me well, Cormac."

He snorted and looked over at Eithne to make sure she was not paying attention. Or refuting Orlaith's desire to leave. When after a few seconds she did neither, Cathal nodded.

"To the tavern we go," he said. "As long as you are up to it."

Eithne raised her head and nodded in unison. "It may not be a bad thing that you get your legs moving. The poison took hold quickly, but your body is strong. As is your soul. You were fighting. And you will need to continue to fight as you recover these next few days."

Orlaith, suddenly conscious of her darkened hand, put it behind her arm. She did not want to show off the fact that she was not healed. She knew her body would take care of it, but it pressed in the back of her mind that something was not right. This was no ordinary bite and therefore would be no ordinary recovery.

Yet, she did not say that, and instead nodded her head in agreement.

"See, Cormac, we can go slow, and if I need to turn around, we will."

He nodded, grabbed her hand, and they began to walk through the door to collect Darragh from the tavern where it all started between the three of them.

CHAPTER 41

$\mathcal{D}$arkness crackled from the king's hands, dripping down like honey. It was slow at first—the dark power—as he stretched his limbs and felt the power began to course. Yet as it neared his fingertips, it began to fall rapidly like waves, the shadows of his power rippling so slowly as he brought himself closer and closer to finding the queen. He knew from his scouts outside of the Criostal castle that they had left.

Was she running from him? Or was she running toward *it*?

They were the Kings of Teine and the Queen of Criostal. The ones who ran. He had known it the moment he had looked upon them, despite Ahren being in their way. Ahren had been despicable, the way he had been ruling as a mere placeholder, and those around him clung to his power. He was merely riding the wave himself, Ahren, and it had been a blessing to the world that the dark king's hands had been the thing to remove him from the world.

A pair that would bring about the end of all of the worlds—his turmoil—if he let them.

He had to find them. There was no other option than this truth.

His shadows reached and reached for Cathal, for his blood ran the closest to Ahren's. The dagger which had done the deed sat across from the king in his make-shift dark throne, all ruby jewels decorating the hilt. The blade was short and dark, made darker by the elven king's blood, and served as a beacon for the king to find Cathal Ambrisona.

There was extreme pain surrounding the boy that the king could not place. His gaze filled with a darkness different from his own when he tried to channel the power necessary to find and place him on the continent.

Something—or someone—was blocking his power beyond the wraith king's vision.

It was maddening. *For what could be more powerful than the king of darkness itself?*

With a demonic hiss, the wraith king stood and threw the dagger with all of his might. It glistened across the chamber as it soared, cutting through the air more beautifully than any shadow had before, and landed in the dark marble wall with a sickening crunch.

The wraith hissed, moving toward it suspiciously, for there were not many blades that could bring about a wound to the castle of Teine like this. As he approached the object, it began to ring in his ears. Screaming wildly, the wraith king flew backward, removing himself from the object entirely. Cursing the knife for all that it was, he fled from the room and vowed to find another way to find the new King of Teine.

And next time, he would not fail.

CHAPTER 42

CATHAL

*D*arragh was completely and utterly obliterated.

In any other circumstance, Cathal would have been ecstatic.

They could have had a round together at the tavern, cheering, dancing, wooing women—rather, Cathal would have been doing the wooing, Darragh would have been an excellent wingman—but this . . . No, this was very bad.

Slumped over the tavern bar side with an ale in hand, Cathal's astute half-brother was nearly unrecognizable in comparison to who he was normally.

"Fuck," Cathal growled, lurching over the masses of people crowded in the tavern to get to him. He could feel Orlaith on his side, a shadow, as they moved toward him in unison.

"Does this happen often?" Orlaith groaned out, moving with him steadily, even though he could sense through her change in body language that the wolf bite still challenged her at every step.

"What are you referencing exactly?" he asked, his eyes darting to her to check on her state. She seemed fine, so he dodged the next person and waited for her to follow.

"Darragh. His current state," she groaned as she followed him.

"No," Cathal hissed as he reached forward to grab hold of his slumped brother. "Dar—Dar, can you hear me?"

Darragh groaned in response, his face soft as though he were sleeping.

Gods, how much did he drink? Did my conversation with him earlier seriously send him onto this bender as such?

"Alright, off we go, Dar," he grunted, heaving him to his feet.

Resting his arm on top of his, Darragh leaned into him fully.

"Orlaith," Cathal barked, suddenly realizing his tone after the fact. He could almost see the rage in her face at the recognition that he had spoken to a queen like that.

Well, your fucking majesty, I wear a crown too.

"Yes, your highness," she hissed through clenched teeth.

Yeah, she was mad.

"How can I be of service?"

"Help me move these people," he said as he grunted again. "I did not mean to—"

"I know," she whispered, her eyes tired and her voice low. Remarkably, he heard her among the yells of the drunken crowd. Turns out there were perks to being a high elf.

With hands spread, the crowd shifted as she walked

through them. She was a queen through and through, people moving out of her way without even a blink. They did not know who she was, yet they bowed to her anyway.

As they neared the doorway, Cathal could feel the wind shifting within the tavern. It was cold, bitter, and somehow attached to a sadness Cathal could identify. It was eerie and familiar all the same. So low that Orlaith probably did not notice that he said it.

Cathal whispered in Darragh's ear, "Are you doing this?"

Darragh groaned out a *no* in response, and suddenly Cathal became very, very aware of the fact that he could see his breath upon his lips.

"Shit," he whispered. "Dar, I need you to walk with me a little better—"

And then he felt it. Piercing pain erupted in his ears, and he could do nothing but scream. He knew this type of noise; he had felt it before. His blood ran cold, his chest tightened.

He could not fucking take a deep breath.

Orlaith was on him in a nanosecond. "Cathal?" she whispered, so nobody would hear his true name. "Cathal, are you alright?"

"It is—" he started to say, slumping over as they exited the door into the Haversin street. "The . . . Wraith . . . King . . . ”

He knew it. That same power that had been there when his grandfather was murdered before his very eyes existed and breathed once more.

On his knees, he had no choice but to drop Darragh as he tried to regain himself. With both hands, Orlaith grabbed his face and put her forehead to his own.

"Breathe with me," she commanded. Always a queen. "In and out. In and out. In and out."

And he did.

With each breath, he felt himself come back. It was slow at first, the relief. But the turquoise gaze of the Queen of Criostal was grounding within itself. There was no more pain, no more sharp noise, and the exhaustion crept from his bones.

With every breath he took and every word of encouragement she said, the Queen of Criostal was washing away the darkness of the Wraith King's infiltration.

No longer weary, he grunted and crawled to Darragh, who was laying in the dirt like a dead body. With a groan, he and Orlaith hoisted him up, his weight manageable between the two of them.

He could tell Orlaith wanted to ask him more about what had affected him, but he knew this was not the place. This was not the time. And he was not even sure what it was to say. He knew it was the Wraith King, somehow and someway. It was the same feeling which had presided over him during the attack on his grandfather, except more short-lived.

He could feel that coldness—and those fucking shadows —coming to him over and over. Lapping at him like it was the sea, and he was merely a stone in its wake.

But what did it all mean? Why was the feeling returning? Why was he being watched? And how did he know? The certainty was unparalleled, for he would not have thrown out an accusation like that without knowing.

With his thoughts clouded and his mind as heavy as Darragh's limp body, they approached the apothecary slowly.

He had been so lost in thought that he had not considered how far out they had been from where they were going.

As they shoved open the door, Cathal noticed once again how pale Orlaith was. Shit, he needed to get both of them upstairs . . .

And then he saw it.

Her *hand*. But in the light this time, and up close.

"Orlaith—" he started, fear coating his voice more so than it ever had.

Noticing that he saw her hand, Orlaith repositioned her hand so he could not see it anymore. "It is healing," she muttered as they began to ascend the staircase.

Unconvincing.

Cathal knew as well as anyone that her darkened hand was far from healing. It looked like plague, a permanent reminder of the wound and the infliction that had happened to her.

Her curse. He knew it. Did she? He had mentioned it before, but did she really understand the implications of a wolf bite?

"Orlaith . . .Eithne can take a look at it," he offered.

"I am fine," she barked with a grunt, as they continued up the stairs together. "I do not need anyone's help."

Cathal sighed, knowing how far that truth was for both of them. And if the roles were reversed, he would not allow another set of eyes to look upon his greatest weaknesses, either. Like everything else, he pushed it away.

As they entered the room and laid down Darragh, Cathal looked down at him sadly. He knew why this had happened, why he drank himself into a stupor.

Cathal had commanded him to do the unthinkable. And Cathal knew what it was to have to do something you did not want to do.

But he knew he could not and would not be the one to tell Orlaith what the necklace was going to curse him to do. There was no way around it.

As he turned around to thank Orlaith for helping tonight, he realized she had already made it over to the bed which she had slept in prior. Turned the other direction, he did not know if she was asleep, but figured she was in no mood to talk, regardless.

Making his way over stealthily, he grabbed a blanket which sat at the end of her bed and draped it over her body. He realized in this moment how normal she looked. How peaceful. She was always so powerful, so commanding in presence, that Cathal seemed to forget to look past the legend and see her for what she truly was.

A girl.

CHAPTER 43

CATHAL

*C*athal went downstairs, ensured Eithne was asleep, and cried.

He was not sure how long he was downstairs, how long he cried for, or even how long he had needed to do this and had not. The release was toxic, embarrassing, and yet it was healing. Hot tears dripped down his face as he hid his head in his hands. It had been years—probably since the death of Michael—that Cathal had sat and done *this*.

A proper cry.

Head pounding, he closed his eyes and tried to wish away all that he had loved and lost. Michael, Ahren, his freedom to choose anything, his life as a prince, his friendship with Orlaith when she would inevitably find out about the necklace, Darragh's soul if he failed . . . It was all too fucking much.

He rocked back and forth—a coping mechanism Darragh had taught him—and he dreamt of a simpler time.

A time where a crown did not sit perfectly atop his head.

A time where Darragh's life was not hanging in the balance.

A time where Orlaith was merely a figment of everyone's imagination, the Queen of Light and Crystals no more an idea rather than a budding friend.

A time where mythical creatures were simply mythical, and the elves were the most to be feared in the name of power.

Breathing deeper, he tried to refocus and reset. Breathing through these bouts of panic was like lighting a fuse and watching it detonate. And in order to heal, he knew he needed to obliterate. Completely and utterly level whatever the world had thrown at him and grovel with it until he understood his role in this.

As if in answer, white hair appeared in his peripheral vision. "Cormac?" she whispered, knowing their identity still had to remain a secret.

But he knew she was asking him, *Cathal? Are you OK?*

"Just having a moment." *No, I am not OK.*

"It happens." *It is OK to feel things.*

"Not for me." *Royals do not feel things, do you not know that?*

"We can change that, you know, the two most powerful elves on the continent."

"I like you better when you speak in riddles."

"Then how about this—why do you fear for me?"

"What?" he asked, genuinely shocked at the question. "Whatever do you mean?"

"When you saw this earlier," Orlaith whispered, raising her gray hand in front of his wet face. "The look in your eye was not unlike the look you had when you saw him in the tavern slumped over."

Cathal snorted, wiping his face on the top of his sleeve. "Darragh does not really drink."

"You are avoiding the question, klutz."

Sighing, Cathal felt the weight of the necklace all too well. It was so damn heavy for being so small. He touched it then, a heat between his fingers ravenous for dark deeds. It was as if the damn thing was alive and telling him that he had to do it. But looking into the sea-glass girl's eyes, he could not.

He would not.

Darragh needed to do it.

If he ever shook off that hangover. He would have had to drink so much—

"You are doing it again," her voice said softly, yet fiercely. "That thing when you look off like you are a lost puppy. What are you thinking about?"

How I am going to have to kill you. "Stuff."

She rolled her eyes, sitting beside him and uncharacteristically putting her head on his shoulder.

"What are you doing?" he asked, unable to hide the surprise in his voice.

"Despite your annoying tendencies, I guess you are still my fiancé until we get what I need."

He nearly went sick at the thought of what would happen if he did get what he needed.

"I guess so," he settled on after an awkward pause.

"Is it so bad, having someone to lean on, Cathal Ambrisona?"

No, he decided after a moment. *But it can be deadly.*

CHAPTER 44

DARRAGH

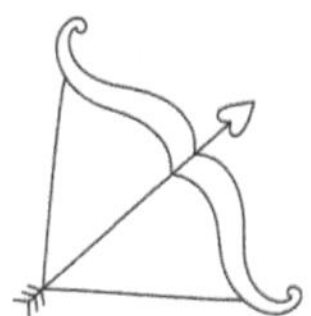

The morning came and Darragh vomited. Shoulders shaking, he heaved himself to his feet. Cursing his lineage, he suddenly felt more human than he ever had before. It was the curse of not being a high-elf, for he was a bastard. Being a high-elf was a privilege, someone born of royalty fully and blessed by the Gods.

And as if Darragh could ever forget—which he could not —he was, in fact, a bastard. And nobody reminded him of it that was of importance to him, for Cathal never reminded him that he was merely his half-brother. Not that Darragh would ever admit it to Cathal, but he felt as though that separation between their stations actually made them stronger together.

But before he could explore the thought, he pushed it away.

Not now would he think about that.

Never, if he had anything to do with it.

Cathal was his brother, and that was all there was to it.

Head spinning, he made his way down the stairs slowly. With a hand over his right temple, he braced himself emotionally for the berating that he was about to receive from Cathal. Frankly, he deserved it. He hoped it was quick and without too many profanities. It had been a long couple of weeks, and he did not know if he could withstand it.

When he reached the bottom of the stairs, however, he found that it was none other than the Queen of Criostal standing in the way of his path.

Fantastic.

This was far worse than anything Cathal could unleash upon him.

"Your Majesty," he grumbled, silently thanking the Gods he was so pale that he could not possibly blush.

She was in his face immediately, nearly a centimeter from her nose touching his own. Her eyes—so tired and weak the other night—were now filled with that familiar blue fire.

If looks could kill, Orlaith Kearan would be a murderer.

He was terrified.

She was terrifying.

And he could not inhale a proper breath.

"You," she growled, lifting a hand covered in a leather glove to point at him.

Looking down, he noticed both of her hands were covered, her dress an equally intimidating yet simple black gown. Probably Eithne's.

It did not make her any less stunning.

"Me?" he asked, terrified of drawing a breath and inhaling another bout of her intoxicating scent.

In an answer, she grabbed the collar of his tunic and dragged him outside of the apothecary. He looked up, noticing the light drizzle and the dark clouds that loomed over them like an omen of death. Clearly, he had woken up later than he had intended. Was it morning still?

She stuck out like a sore thumb in this place, even in her ordinary clothes. Her white hair, ethereal in its own nature, was a force to be reckoned with among even the most beautiful of elves.

With a snarl, she knocked him out of his stupor as she shoved him against the dark wall, her arm pinning him. Momentarily, the wind was knocked out of him. All of his wind. Even if he could summon it. Though, he could not help but acknowledge that he was powerless against anything she would do.

But that was all he would let him admit to himself.

Nothing more.

"You hurt him," she hissed.

This was about fucking Cathal? Just and Mercy, did she not feel it too—

"What?" he asked, finding it hard again to take a deep breath. She had quite the grip.

"I should not even tell you this, a betrayal of my fiancé's confidence, but he was a mess last night, Darragh. I found him slumped on the floor of the apothecary, completely and utterly alone, because you decided, for whatever reason, to be an idiot!" She was raising her voice, and people were definitely staring. He could tell she did not care.

"Cathal?" he asked, his heart suddenly weighing all too much.

"Yes. Do you remember him? Your brother? Your fucking King?"

Darragh gulped. He was never the reason for Cathal's panic. Never. *What had changed?*

Rolling her eyes, Orlaith released him with a huff. Something was still off about her, something different regarding the way she was carrying herself. It was like something had switched between her getting attacked and now, but based upon the way she had shoved him against the wall, clearly, she did not know—

He opened his mouth to ask when she lifted a gloved finger to hush him. "When you see him, you say nothing of this."

Darragh nodded.

"And when you talk to him, you apologize for being an idiot. I do not care what caused it—"

You.

Cathal thinks he has to kill you. Or I die.

And he will not take no for an answer.

"But your brother does not deserve that. And frankly, neither do I." She turned back toward the apothecary, her head turning over her shoulder as she said in finality, "And do it now, so we can go and get my crown."

Darragh's heart sunk in his chest, and even though it was misplaced, a fire built within him.

"They worship you, you know? Your kingdom," his voice was wavering, unsteady.

She huffed a laugh, refusing to make eye contact with him in this moment. "Stop trying to change the subject, Darragh. This is not about me."

"That is what you do not understand! It is *always* about you!"

She shirked backward, clearly misinterpreting what he was saying.

Gods, did he even know what he was saying?

"I did not mean to hurt Cathal," he whispered, unable to find the words he needed to say.

This was his chance, his shot to come clean about what was going on. They could not keep her from the crown. They were bringing her to it, but they did not want to bring her to her doom. They had been hoping these two scenarios were separate from one another, but as they approached and tensions heightened, Darragh was beginning to realize this was an impossible feat.

"I know," she said sadly, looking far less fierce than she had moments before when she had nearly attacked him.

"Your kingdom—" he restarted, taking the window to try again. Maybe this time, he could find the words. "Growing up in Teine, in this place, we heard a lot of rumors about you, Orlaith."

"The mysterious ruler with the light," she said, rolling her eyes.

"Royal rumors, of course, but I think there is some truth to it beyond the scope of power," Darragh said, choosing his words carefully. She was listening and was not combating him; it was now or never.

Kneeling down at her feet, he gazed upward at her. "You bring a light, beyond that of a blast of power, Orlaith. Cathal and I might have saved you with the wolven, but it is you that has shown us the light—the way of things—beyond what we thought we knew."

For once, she was speechless.

So, he continued, taking advantage of a few more moments with her. Alone. What could he say without giving it all away? Without taking down the world?

Not breaking eye contact, he said, "Let them pray."

"What?" she asked, confused by the intensity of his—well—everything.

"Let them pray. Let them fall at your feet: men, women, elves, wolven—whomever. Let them continue to worship the idea of you, to live in fear of you if that is what it takes." Rising to meet her gaze, he now stood over her and gazed down at her. A power play within itself, but one he knew she would be receptive to.

Leaning so closely to her, he knew she could feel his hot breath against the side of her cheek. "I am not fine with the back and forth. You are either with Cathal and myself, or you are against us."

There it was, the challenge he knew she would understand. It was not honesty, or to even unveil the truth to her, that Orlaith needed to rise to the occasion. Darragh could not find the words, but he could convey everything without using them.

A chance he was willing to take to have the other half of his soul hear him.

Truly hear him.

"And how would you know if I am with you?" she growled, turquoise eyes blazing.

"I would not," he said back with a smirk. "I guess that is the fun of being royal. It all comes down to trust and prayer."

Without another word, she turned from him, her white hair flowing in the wind that had picked up senselessly. She was pissed, completely and utterly pissed. And when he opened his mouth to unveil a little more, to tell her so that Cathal would no longer be burdened and manic, he found that nothing came.

It may have been the most selfish moment of Darragh's life.

He did nothing but slide down the wall of the apothecary's outside as she walked away. Letting the moment pass him by as she disappeared down the streets of Criostal.

CHAPTER 45

ORLAITH

W ham.

The door to the apothecary slammed shut behind her as she made her way back inside. The day was colder than she was used to, as if the land itself was shaking itself up and preparing to lose everything for the crown.

She sighed, the weight of everything overbearingly heaving against her chest.

It started today. Her path toward getting what was rightfully hers. To getting what her father had laid before her and had been taken. Whatever bargain he had struck with the wolven, whatever secrets had been harbored, and whatever existed in this world as a result of the crown being lost—it was about to be over.

With a glance down at her dark gloved hand, Orlaith felt a prickle of uneasiness wash over her. Inch by inch, her bones grew colder, and she could hear her own heartbeat speeding up. It thundered in her chest, threatening to rupture as she took in the knowledge that she already knew.

She silently forbade it to even cross her mind; the thought was so damning she knew the second it touched her tongue, everything she had ever dreamed of would be destroyed.

"It is not getting better, is it?" A voice sounded from the corner of the room so quietly Orlaith was almost alarmed she had not heard it.

Inhaling a sharp breath, Orlaith said nothing.

It was a silent answer.

A prayer.

A hope.

An admittance.

And a damnation.

"I will not say anything," Eithne said sadly. "I feared the poison had gone too far, but when you woke up . . . Well, I thought, you would be fine."

"I am fine," Orlaith forced out. Unable to accept anything other than that.

"Yes," Eithne whispered, digging around her shelves for a vile. *The* vile, Orlaith supposed. "I suppose you will be."

Orlaith opened her mouth and shut it, for Eithne was speaking once more.

"Are you familiar with a wolven curse?" Her widened eyes were all that Eithne needed. Sucking in a breath of surprise, her hand flew over her mouth. "You knew nothing then?"

Orlaith snorted and replied honestly, "I was educated to the highest degree, yet I suppose I learned nothing of true importance."

"Did you ever feel it, a weight? A darkness?"

Orlaith thought back to her life in flashes and tried to remember a time when darkness had overcome her. And all that came to mind was the wolven attacking her, revealing some truth about a deal her father made.

Shuddering, she shook her head. She could not possibly describe it to Eithne. She would not understand.

Nobody would.

She paused and Orlaith stiffened. She did not do well in conversations of substance on a normal day, but to be here with Eithne made her feel something different. She was thinking, a start to growing, she supposed. Eithne was warm, loving, so much like fucking Dealla that Orlaith's heart nearly ripped in two.

She had done a good job recently of pushing it away—all of the pain that clawed at her and hurt worse than a wolf bite. It had been easy to throw everything she had into her conversation with Darragh. He was easy to fight with, despite the fact that he did not push as she pulled.

It had felt good to be angry at something. To channel it.

But Eithne had the same power Dealla did, the power to take the whole wall that Orlaith had built up and bring it the fuck down. That much was certain.

Without warning, Eithne stepped closer to Orlaith, her gaze filled with worry and admiration all at once. So close in proximity, her voice was merely a whisper as she said, "I can only assume who you are, your Majesty. And I am truly,

truly, sorry you did not know what weights you carried with you."

Orlaith stiffened, but did not let the scent of fear waft off her. She held her breath: deathly still and lethally calm.

"And I will not tell a soul, not your Cormac or anyone else." She winked. She actually winked. "But I need to you to know, your Majesty, that I have been a healer a long time. Longer than you would even imagine. And I have only seen a few wolf bites during that time—"

"I already know what you are going to say, and I forbid you to say it." Orlaith's voice was commanding. Stern. The voice of a queen.

Eithne paused, her skin turning a shade lighter as she took in Orlaith's command.

Wiping a single tear from her cheek, Orlaith allowed herself one inhale of a shuddering breath. It was anything less than perfection—and it was completely unacceptable—but Eithne had that quality Dealla had.

Devastatingly understanding.

And brutally loyal.

And perfectly honest.

She allowed herself this one moment, this one feeling, for just a second before she asked, "How long?"

"It is impossible to say, your Majesty. But things will become more progressive. This exhaustion that I can see on you is only the start. The darkness will spread. Your elven body will fight it off, but this is all I can promise. I have never seen it in junction with a curse. The end will come, and it will be painful. The supplements will help—"

"How can you see this curse on me? Do I wear it like a gown?" All sarcasm was void in her voice.

"There is almost like a cloud around you, your energy and aura wafted by something both greater and darker." Eithne's eyes were sad. "There are peaks of light, bursts I see that fight off the darkness around you, but it proves fruitless. Even now, as we were speaking, I could see you fighting it off."

"Will I be able to put it on?" Orlaith's voice was all ice. All sadness gone. Evaporated. And all that was left in its wake was desperation.

And maybe a twinge of rage.

"Your Majesty, you have all of the fight within you. I think that is the reason you have come this far, to live this long with a curse of this magnitude . . . You are nothing but a spectacle for us all," Eithne said, her dark eyes swarming with emotion that Orlaith refused to acknowledge.

"Will. I. Be. Able. To. Put. It. On?" She was an inch from her face, intimidating as all of the hells she could imagine.

"I do not know," Eithne said after a pause. She understood. She got what Orlaith was asking at her core.

Would her body survive the transfer of power from the crown to the Isle? What was going to happen to her if she could not hold on, if the crown did not accept someone who was doomed?

Orlaith closed her eyes and breathed out from her nose so deeply she was surprised smoke was not exuding from her. She was this close, and now everything threatened to fall away from her.

Cursed she was indeed.

"I dismiss you, Eithne," Orlaith said as she began to walk up the staircase. She needed to be alone. Completely and utterly alone. For just a minute—

"Your Majesty—" Eithne whispered, but Orlaith kept walking. She did not need to hear what she had to say. She needed nothing.

Nothing she could get back.

CHAPTER 46

DARRAGH

Orlaith had knocked the wind out of him. It was not every day that an elf's anam told them they had royally fucked up.

And he had, he knew it.

And he had messed up again by not saying anything to her in that very moment, the opportunity to tell her everything.

Yet, he was at her mercy. He was on his knees for her before he even knew what was happening, before he knew they were to be engaged in conversation. She had choked him against a fucking wall, yet here he was unable to speak because of the effect she had on him.

He had told her to let the people of this world pray to her, but it was really he who was praying he could fix everything. That he could somehow find a way to keep her alive.

He was destroyed. She had destroyed him without doing much of anything. Is this what it was to be the other half of someone's soul? To be lingering always and struggle to formulate anything around them of substance? To be bent and strung in whichever way the other commanded? It was maddening.

He did not know how to handle what he needed to do. He had never been this lost. The lines blurred endlessly between what he knew was the truth of this world—duty, kingdom lines—everything was wrong. Everything was broken.

He was not who he was when he left the castle of Teine.

And he was no longer sure if that was a good or a bad thing.

In stride with his brother, they walked along the streets of Haversin twice with no conversation between them. Cathal had walked outside and joined him silently, as if he already knew something Darragh did not. The silence was deafening, an unspoken way about them which was so heavy that neither of them seemed capable of speaking first.

Darragh opened his mouth—finally—but per usual, Cathal beat him to it.

"I could not tell her," Cathal said with an eerie sense of calm. "She was right in front of me earlier, and I could do nothing but talk to her about anything else. I tried, Darragh. I tried to ease you of this."

"There has to be another way," Darragh whispered.

And that was it. The reason he had not said anything, the reason he got so drunk. He was trying to buy himself—and her—time from learning this truth. "This curse around your neck cannot be the end all to what Ahren wanted you to do. There has to be another way. A way around it—"

"We are leaving later, Dar." Cathal's voice was shaking. Clearly, Darragh was not the only one who was affected by this. "And she is going to put it on her head. She deserves to meet this destiny, to reclaim what Grandfather stole from her."

"But when she puts it on . . ."

Cathal touched his necklace, his hands shaking so slightly that only Darragh would notice. He was on the verge of panic; it was clear as day to him. But Darragh let him continue, let him work through it on his own terms and time. This was a conversation that must be had, and Darragh did not need to hold his brother's hand through this.

"Holding me back is not an option, Darragh."

Darragh knew what this meant. Him dying. That would be the cost.

Darragh was not willing to pay up.

"We will have a day's ride to Alexandriti when we leave Haversin, Caw. We will have a day to figure it out."

"A day. You truly think we can figure this out in a day?"

Darragh ran a hand over his long scar, and Cathal's eyes widened in surprise. Darragh never touched the wound, never acknowledged it, so this was an admittance. And a promise.

"This comes down to survival, and I will make sure she does just that."

CHAPTER 47

ORLAITH

They set out at dawn the next morning.

Orlaith blinked as Haversin slowly made its way out of her line of sight and sighed. No longer was she in her kingdom.

"Sad to go so soon?" Cathal asked, his horse pacing in front of hers. They had taken another horse from Eithne—or rather, she had given it to them—so Orlaith did not need to ride with one of the boys.

She could not possibly ride with Cathal; he was completely and utterly insufferable. She would not tolerate it.

She could not possibly ride with Darragh, either, for whatever had passed between them during and after the wolven attack had changed some innate chemistry between them. And she would not, and could not, be a subject to do so again.

Not until she had a crown.

Not until she unveiled the secrets her father had left in the wake of his death.

Her father's death was something she was at peace with. She had made peace with it so many years before. She had never met him, but she could not deny the moments in the last nineteen years where she could have sworn he was there. Whether it was the way of the wind, the smells of the castle . . . he was there. She knew it. He had to be.

Coming back to herself after what she was sure was an extensive pause, she replied, "I have never left Criostal before of my own accord."

Cathal raised a dark eyebrow. "What?"

"Who would have taken me? The Maester of Horses?" She laughed, and Cathal cracked a wry smile. "I have never left Criostal of my own accord because nobody has ever taken me from Criostal."

"I have been more places than I care to admit," Cathal said softly, his dapple horse trotting closer to her own. "But that does not make me any more worthy of being a royal, if that is what you are thinking."

"I was not," she said with a smirk. "But thanks for planting the thought in my head."

He laughed, but his gaze remained full of something Orlaith could not place. *Was it guilt? What in the name of the Gods could he have to be guilty about—*

"Orlaith—" he started, gripping the reins so tightly Orlaith was sure she was seeing things.

There was no way in the name of the Gods that Cathal Ambrisona was terrified of anything. Of saying anything. He was the klutz. He was the one whose eyes were always twinkling.

It was Darragh who was all darkness and secrets.

"We need to keep moving if we want to make it to Alexandriti before dark falls," his fucking voice cut through the air like Oidhe did her enemies.

And it was nonetheless Darragh who was interrupting them right now.

She opened her mouth to nearly snarl at him, to breathe fire into him and demand he go away for another moment so his brother could let down the mask for a second.

Cathal, clearly, was done with what he was about to say.

Regrettably.

"Cathal—" she tried, asking twice.

She could not command it out of him to tell her what he wanted to say, but he was already galloping away after Darragh's midnight horse.

Rolling her eyes, she encouraged her horse to take a step over the border. And for the first time in her life, she was a monarch in a foreign land.

It seemed as though this was a day of firsts.

A few hours after breaking away from the line, Orlaith could feel the wariness in her bones for the first time in her life. She knew without removing her gloves that it was her hand, the wolf bite and curse seeming to have a mind of its own so strong that she was beginning to lose whatever magic made her immortal.

Whatever it was that made her an elf, it was dissipating.

As the minutes dragged on—her bones more brittle by the moment, and her head beginning to lull—she knew she was running out of time. She had to get to the crown, formulate a plan, and fast.

Cathal had told her before they departed that the crown lay in his grandfather's chambers. It would be very well guarded, but he was the king now. And the king had to bow to nobody.

It would be strategic, she figured, and a lot easier than she had anticipated her whole life after imagining going through this with Ahren. But with Ahren out of the way, Cathal would not stand in her way.

As he had been explaining to her prior to leaving—with Darragh very silently stewing in the corner—he was on board with her decision to wear the crown. And if worse came to worst, they were engaged.

Her kingdom, by all accounts, would fall to him.

Discreetly, she had managed to get that approved by the Maesters upon her departure from Criostal. Maybe that was why it was so difficult to cross that border hours ago, because she knew there was a chance she would never come back. Her beloved kingdom, filled with the Isle's most beautiful flowers and gems unlike most had ever seen, humans and elves who lived in harmony, and a pride within themselves to always be righteous. That was what existed in her kingdom. That was who her father had demanded his people be.

Completely and utterly kind.

But her mind went back to the plague that attacked the lands, the impending war since the kingdom had been ravaged by the crown, taking the life of Prince Michael and refusing to give it back. It was wrong, all of it. And the Isle had paid the ultimate price as a result of the thievery.

A thievery she was to rectify.

Today.

"Thinking about something?"

With a spin of her head, she met Darragh's darkened gaze. His scar seemed more permanent today, standing out on his devastatingly gorgeous face. His auburn hair was glistening in the sunlight, though the clouds left him shrouded and darkened his other features.

"My head is not filled with air," she said simply.

Hurt flashed across his face, and Orlaith felt a wave of nausea overtake her. *Why did she always have to be on the defense?*

"I am worried," she added as he began to trot away. His horse slowed on his command, retreating to be side by side to her own. "I am worried I will never see my kingdom again. I am not sure I can live an eternity without the scent of flowers."

Although she was trying to play off her fear, she could tell Darragh was having none of it. "I am hopeful you will live an eternity, Orlaith."

Surprise flashed across her face, despite her best efforts to hide it.

"It is me I am worried about," he offered before speeding away to ride beside Cathal.

CHAPTER 48

CATHAL

The ride was quiet as they approached Alexandriti. They had been riding all day, all lost in the same swirl of thoughts.

Despite all three of them being so different, they were very much the same.

As they crested the hillside to what Cathal knew as home, he realized how the castle was different than he remembered, though it was not that many sunrises and sunsets since he saw it last. The outside was darker than he had ever realized before, no longer a stoned gray, but now instead a midnight black. It was as if it were clouded in night itself, as dangerous as the crown which sat inside of it.

He prayed it was the trick of the light, though he knew deep down it was no such thing.

Something was completely and utterly wrong.

As they entered the city of Alexandriti, Cathal half expected the people of the citadel to jump forth and greet them. Yet, the streets were empty, besides the clanging of pots hanging outside people's homes and a stray black cat that wandered aimlessly. He knew there were people in their homes, yet the blinds were drawn. *Who—or what—were they hiding from?*

"I know your kingdom is not like mine," Orlaith tread carefully with her words behind them. "But I never heard tales of it that match this."

"It is not normally like this, not at all." Darragh's voice was quiet, as if he were afraid of waking the dead.

"We have been gone too long. Too unstable. Why did the Maesters of Court not—" Cathal was cut off by the sound of screeching. He immediately bent over his horse and tried to shield himself with his wind from the noise. A power he rarely used at his disposal, for he preferred to be as normal as possible at all times. Even though he was anything but normal, he was Cathal. It was deafening. He could not breathe. He could not think—

"Cathal," the voice brought him back. Commanding, yet filled with kindness. Filled with friendship. "Cathal, you do not have to go inside if it is too much."

He lifted his face to see Orlaith, her palms open before him and holding the smallest ball of light he could imagine. It flickered, as if no more a flame that was threatening to go out. Yet, she held it steady as he focused in on it.

And the panic went away.

Blinking up at her, he could vaguely see Darragh in his peripheral. But the concern was etched there, and Darragh could see on his face as plainly as Cathal knew it in his blood.

They were out of time.

And Cathal had spent this entire ride thinking through a plan, which he never figured a loophole around.

Cathal would not lose Darragh.

And Cathal could not kill Orlaith.

Before he brought himself to answer his own question, for he knew the answer, he took a deep breath. *Push it away, push it away, push it away . . .*

After he opened his eyes, he did not look at her. He could not. He only looked at Darragh, a plea, and a silent one at that.

A command to do it.

Darragh nodded slowly, understanding and admitting to Cathal what he could not say.

That he understood.

And he would forgive him.

"We go in, and we get the crown." He swung off his horse smoothly, that elven agility returning to his bones after a momentary lapse in remembering who he was. And what he was capable of.

King Ahren had always called him clever, kind, and worthy.

Well, Cathal was about to show how clever and worthy he was.

And how ruthless he could be.

Orlaith unsheathed her sword, and Cathal nearly looked back at her to make sure she did not sway. He saw her sway on her horse, but he refused to unveil her weakness in front of Darragh. So, per usual, Cathal closed his mouth when he should have opened it.

A hand grabbed his shoulder, fierce and protective. And understanding. "Let us go see what that was—"

Even though they both knew what it was.

Why the people were absent from the village.

He had one guess, and one which he felt in the center of his soul that he was right.

The Wraith King had to be here, and by the looks of it, he was not alone.

CREEPING ALONG, they walked in a triangle formation. Swords raised, ears perked up, and eyes never once leaving in front of them. It was Cathal in the front, insistent. Orlaith and Darragh flanked behind him, rather reluctant not to take the brunt if something were to happen.

If a wraith had destined to reveal itself.

The castle was tarnished, the walls darker, and shadows creeping along as they had when Ahren had been killed. Carefully, they did not touch them out of fear of awakening something bigger and far more terrifying than they even knew what to do with.

Nobody spoke a word, or even dared to encourage one another, out of fear of alerting what they thought was aware they were here. Like most things, if they pretended, they could ignore it.

Gesturing with his hands, Cathal checked every corner and hallway before they made themselves ready to move. The air was peculiar, for this was not the same place he had left weeks before. The halls were darker, his movements slower. It was this fucking necklace, a curse within itself.

He had been thinking of Orlaith this whole time, what this meant for her and how he was going to stop Ahren's magic from taking over. But maybe, just maybe, it was Cathal who needed the curse to be broken after all.

It had been minutes, but Cathal thought it was taking hours. They moved swiftly, their elven feet not making even one move out of line. They had to get to the crown. They had to do that so Cathal could—

And then they were at the door. Cathal put a finger to his lips, ordering all to be quiet as he used his wind to break the key lock.

Orlaith hissed, cursing.

He looked back at her with a wink. "What? Did you think you were the only one with gifts, Orlaith?"

Darragh groaned. "You are the only elf on the Isle who could be making jokes right now, Cathal."

"My specialty," Cathal said with a smirk.

With a quiet slicing, it was off. And the door swung open.

And there it was.

Orlaith put a hand over her mouth to stop herself from gasping, for the power the crown beheld was magnificent to him without any attachment to the damned thing. If anything, he hated how it had cleaved his family into parts.

He was glad to be rid of it, and to use its power for good instead of evil. Orlaith could do it. She could put everything back together.

She could put the world back together.

Putting an arm out, Cathal refused to let them go forth without his inspection. They had somehow made it in here too quickly, too softly, without even a hiccup. Darragh knew it too, for his gaze was so clouded that Cathal was becoming concerned about the permanent frown encroaching on his forehead.

Once they stilled, though Orlaith had not even moved an inch, he stepped forward. He looked to the left and then to the right, and when the coast was clear, he stepped through the threshold of the door—

And then Cathal tripped over his own two feet, and the whole world exploded into chaos.

CHAPTER 49

DARRAGH

Cathal was a fucking idiot.

The screaming started first, then the shadows erupted. The crown's visibility lost to the sound of the wraith's fast approach. They had to get down, they had to get down, they had to get down—

And explosion rocked them. Cathal was screaming, and Darragh realized quickly it was not from injury. He searched him feverishly regardless among the shadows that clouded them like smoke.

"I am fine," Cathal gasped. "Get *her* out of here." Cathal's hands shook violently, and Darragh knew he had seconds to move before Cathal did the unthinkable.

"I am sorry, brother, but I cannot let you do this," Darragh said with a growl, his feral nature taking complete control. Unsheathing his dagger, Darragh flipped it around to its hilt, and in one fell swoop hit Cathal in the temple with it.

With a thud, Cathal hit the floor of the castle of Teine, unconscious.

Without a second glance, Darragh was already moving. He knew what Cathal would do and what would happen if he . . . But it appeared that Orlaith was equally moving. On her forearms, she was crawling for it. The crown so close, her entire destiny before her.

Darragh ran. Fast.

"ORLAITH!" he screamed, his heart pounding.

The crown's draw was strong. If he could grab her hand, maybe he could stop her just for a moment to explain—

"ORLAITH!" he screamed again, Isle-shattering pain erupting through his ears as the wraiths got closer and closer.

Behind him, he heard the unsheathing of a sword and readied himself for battle against the creatures.

"Orlaith," he tried one more time, softer. As he caught up to her on his hands and knees, he touched her arm softly. "Or—"

She stopped, just for a moment. Tears stained her beautiful face, her turquoise eyes nearly puffy from the emotions and years of hurt that tore down her face. He could not do this. He could not breathe—

"I am ready for this, Darragh. I am ready—"

"Please," he whispered. It was a silent plea, one he so desperately needed to say. He had waited too long, but he had to try.

She paused for a second. A second long enough. Maybe there was a deeper connection between them after all.

Darragh grabbed the Queen of Criostal by her shoulders and shouted, "If you put it on, Cathal is going to kill you!"

She went green. Her turquoise eyes filling with tears so fast again that Darragh was sure they were about to erupt. That she was about to overflow and explode. Lips quivering, she breathed out one word that was filled with so much surprise and sadness that Darragh was not even sure she knew she said it.

"What?"

The words tumbled out, and Darragh could do nothing to stop it. "It is his necklace. Ahren made him wear it. It is an oath. An oath, Orlaith."

She closed her eyes, her hand going to her own throat as if she too were wearing the necklace. As if she could feel its power and pretend to be Cathal for a moment. It was all clicking together in her mind now. He could tell by the furrowing of her brows. The fact that they were all in sync, but could never be harmonious, the hidden motivations . . . It all made sense now.

"An emerald necklace for an emerald curse?" She huffed a laugh, tears spilling down the sides of her cheeks so innocently that Darragh did not know if she knew she was crying. "Ahren always had a sick sense of humor."

"Orlaith—" He had to tell her. He had to tell her everything.

Another scream carried through the dark hall, shadows twirling and threatening to suffocate. But for some reason, they did not reach the two of them crouched in the hallway.

"What are the terms?" she interrupted. "*What are the terms?*"

As she turned, he could see the recognition on her face that he had knocked Cathal out.

"What did you do—"

Darragh inhaled and exhaled slowly. He could do this. He could tell her. He had to. She was *asking*. "When you put it on, Cathal is to kill you."

"And if he does not? Can he resist?"

"My heart will stop beating."

If possible, she went paler than she was before.

One heartbeat.

Two heartbeats.

Three heartbeats.

"Well," she said, leaning so close to him that he nearly closed his own eyes at her smell. It was of roses and steel, ethereal and maddeningly strong.

Suddenly, her lips brushed his, but it was not a kiss.

It was a goodbye.

"Then I better get to it."

And then the whole castle lit up in a flash of light.

CHAPTER 50

ORLAITH

Blinding light exploded from her, the source of her power at its core. And for the first time, this close to the crown, she understood why she had this. For this very moment, among the darkness and shadows.

She was the light.

And may the light guide her toward the crown.

Running, she silently prayed to the Gods that Darragh had closed his eyes, and that Cathal was still unconscious, when she reached the crown. Pausing, she drew Oidhe, and prayed it would not hurt.

And prayed Cathal would know what to do when he woke up.

Hands shaking, she awkwardly turned Oidhe to touch the top of her chest, where her heart would lay. She dreamt for a moment, just a moment, of what she would say to her father and her mother if they met her where she was going, when she heard a voice.

The voice of death itself.

"Orlaith Kearan, how lovely of you to join us."

She did not need to turn around to know who it was, rather *what* it was. The Wraith King. The murderer of King Ahren. And the murderer of Dealla.

But she did anyway, the crown behind her protectively.

"You knew," she said. "You knew who I was this whole time."

"And who might that be, my child?"

"The conduit of your power, your Majesty." She spat the word with ice as he took another ghostly step toward her.

His face was hidden under the shadows he wore, only a crown visible as darkness wafted off his robes.

"This whole time, you have been trying to get me. To take my throne, to conquer my power . . . You have been trying to do this for years. That is why my father made a deal with the wolven, correct?"

He paused, considering. *"Your Majesty, how bold of you to assume you know all of the inner workings of your history without guidance. Without my guidance, you will amount to nothing, Queen of Criostal."*

"I think you need me. That is why I was crowned, how I ascended the throne after my parents died. That is why you murdered Dealla. You were testing the limits of my power, seeing how bright I could shine when provoked."

"How very brilliant of you. My have you grown since you were crowned. It is a shame your father could not see you now."

At the mention of her father, she felt herself slip. "The lands do not die if I die, but you do." Taking a step closer, she continued, "That is why you have not killed me, is it not? My father knew it too, and that is why he made a deal with the wolven to save me. To curse me. For your fate is tied to mine, a way to ensure I will survive this. That I will survive *you*."

"*How bold of you to assume—*"

"There is another. A ruler who is worthy to take my place. It is my destiny as much as it is his." She smirked, knowing she had the Wraith King right where she wanted him. "And he is tied to nothing but my doom."

The king paused, but Orlaith could see it. The shadows flickered. The shadows began to slow.

He was nervous.

Because she was right.

"*Who might that be?*" he asked.

"You walked by him on the way in." She smirked.

Cathal emerged with his sword from the shadows.

Hands shaking, Orlaith could see he was not right. He was fighting off the urge to kill her, a magic bound in the emerald necklace that hung at his neck with such a vengeance that it glowed green. A mockery to her and her power. Her legacy.

It was too bad that Ahren was dead, for in this moment, she wanted to kill him herself.

The king laughed, a dark and nasty cackle so evil that her spine shook. "*Oh, Orlaith, how clever you are. As clever as your father was when he tried to take me for a fool, exchanging his life for yours. It is my understanding that he made quite a few deals before he came begging to me. To save you.*"

"To save me?"

"*Because your fate is sealed, and it is—*"

He did not finish. He could not.

Because Darragh had thrown his grandfather's knife directly into the shadows.

Directly into the Wraith King.

Rubies danced in the darkness, but it was unmistakable. It was the knife that kings had used to murder kings. Red still from what she assumed was Ahren's very own blood.

And it went straight through him, as he began to scream and wail as if he was being dragged down to Hell itself.

As Darragh moved to get closer, to draw another blow with another weapon, Orlaith did not have enough time to draw an inhale as the Wraith King took one final gasp and drove his own knife through Darragh's heart.

CHAPTER 51

DARRAGH

Darragh always wondered what it would feel like to die.

He imagined as a boy there would be pain, some sort of deafening crunch, and an audible connection with the Gods as the soul of the body would join what higher powers there may be.

He learned however, as the knife cut deep within him, that there was only coldness and a haunting sensation to call out to her.

And he could see her now, rushing toward the procession of men, women, and elves who dignified the crowds. He could have sworn he heard her shrieking above all else, yet there was something utterly beautiful about the way it made his blood curdle. He knew he was dreaming, for it had been only Cathal, Orlaith, and the Wraith King with him. But that was what it felt like with the Queen of Criostal, like all things happening were bigger than themselves.

He knew in that moment, and he would forever more, that she cared for him more than he ever knew was possible. And the worst part was, he would have driven his own knife through his heart for her.

But the king beat him to it.

As the breath of life left his lungs, and his head lulled against the concrete floors below him, he tried to whisper the name of the girl who continued to push past the crowds to say goodbye. Though, the thing about death that he now understood was, it was final, and he had nothing more to give.

This vision—whatever had brought it on, or whoever had brought it on—was completely and utterly devastating.

Instead, one word bubbled on his lips as blood began to seep out. He knew now that this part, this vision, was real in some regards. He could feel her reaching for him. He knew she was here, touching him and screaming. For one quick moment, he tried to reach out for Cathal, his one comfort in this world, but instead only found her.

It was always her, he decided then. It would always be her.

And now she would get to live because of him.

One word he told himself he would not utter, a word so ancient in power that the last thing he saw as he whispered it was a flash of light so bright he was sure everyone within miles would go blind.

"Anam," he whispered in his final breath.

EPILOGUE

*O*rlaith was burning, the light within her both true freedom and shackled pain. Her lips collided with Darragh's softly, hesitantly. They were both rutted in their ways, stubborn and unyielding. It took all within her not to smile as she felt him retracting but refused to be the first to yield to her whim.

Her light flared, yet she kept her eyes open. His amber gaze remained hidden amongst the brightness, a refusal to acknowledge both the power she possessed and the emotions they had both buried for so long.

Strong hands gripped her shoulders, and she nearly flung herself at him in order to keep this moment going. Slowly, she saw his bent arms unlock, no longer frozen and welcoming. He was pushing her away slowly, rejecting her.

"No," she hissed. "You do not get to push me away."

The corners of his mouth twitched in amusement. "You are very demanding, did you know that?"

She stepped closer, her breath hot and nearly smoking against his lips once more. "I am a queen."

"You are not my queen."

Titling her head to the side, she whispered, "I could be."

He paused, considering her words carefully before he replied. "Orlaith . . ."

"What is it that keeps your light from shining, Darragh?" She put her shaking hands on his shoulders. "What is it that keeps you from being you?"

"Orlaith, I am the bastard brother of the Kingdom of Teine."

"And does that mean you are not allowed to experience what life has to offer?" she clarified. "What I can be for you? What we can be for one another?"

"It means I cannot be who you need me to be." The golden flecks in his eyes reflected the dark sadness that dwelled within her.

There was an unfortunate truth to his circumstances, but Orlaith refused to believe in the rituals of a society that was broken.

"Who do I need you to be?" She kinked her head to the side. When he did not reply, she whispered, "Darragh . . . You do not get to leave me before I know what this means."

"I need you to rule, to marry my brother, and wear the Emerald Crown. It is what you have always wanted. I saw that clear on your face the first time I came to the castle. You wanted to do anything to get back what is rightfully yours . . ."

"And marrying your brother will help me achieve what I want?" She could barely keep the disbelief out of her voice.

"It is the rightful thing to do. Cathal has a good soul and would bring peace to the Isle in a union with you."

It took all within her not to hit him and scream the obvious. "I do not doubt your idiot brother would be a formidable match. Despite his inability to stand up straight and not bother me, I have become very fond of him these last few weeks."

Darragh nearly sagged, yet Orlaith pretended not to notice.

She continued, "But I do not see a scenario in which it would bring either of us inexplicable joy. If I am the one to wear the Emerald Crown, it very well may take my life if I am not chosen by the Gods."

He took a deep, painful breath in reply to her damning truth.

"And if I am to die, who would I entrust my kingdom? I believe he would be a fair king and a just one, but he is not where my heart lies."

She stepped away from Darragh, her hands sweaty and rubbing against the side of her red velvet gown. Her voice was anything but steady as she whispered, "But if you were to stay, my kingdom would fall to you should the crown take me. And I can think of nobody else worthy to run my kingdom as I would."

"I cannot accept such a—"

Closing the gap between them, she softly kissed his bottom lip and cut him off from saying more. "Think about it. For me."

He nodded so subtly she was sure if she thought of the action again she would deem that she made it up.

"Come back to me," she whispered. *"Come back to me, anam."*

—

Darragh knew he was dreaming. *Is this what death was? A mere dream?*

And he knew he was dead the second his eyes flew open.

Mist and shadow clouded around him in an array of complete chaos, whispering winds that curled and shirked themselves around his bloodied body as he came to. Gasping for air, he rolled over, his eyes nearly rolling back into his head again when he saw the king of the wraiths step forward.

He was not like he was when he drove the knife through King Ahren's heart. Rather, he was more humanistic, his hands discernible and his darkness somehow more terrifying. He was real, more-so than he had been. The crown of the deceased atop his head was made of elven bones.

How Darragh knew this was yet to be determined, but he knew it all the same.

Tremors floated up his spine, and he began to shake uncontrollably. But he was fucking dead? Why was he still cold?

"You are not dead, heir to the ashen throne," the Wraith King whispered in a hiss that sounded only like death could.

Just and Mercy—

"Just and Mercy, and none of your other silly little Gods can help you now, Darragh. There is only what I want and what I need."

"Then what do you want?" he asked, his teeth chattering incessantly.

Terror ripped through him. His scar burned. He could have sworn he was dead—

"*I need you to tell me everything about the Queen of Criostal*," he said, leaning down with a wicked smile. "*Now, tell me, how bright is that light of hers, after all?*"

ACKNOWLEDGMENTS

The book kinda came to me in a wild dream and chaotic sense, which for me means it came to be completely naturally and utterly normally. Picture this: me on my couch in my old apartment (please remember that Will calls this couch to this day a glorified chair), my two cats inches from my head, drinking kombucha from a wine glass, and watching Lord of the Rings for the ten millionth time. I thought to myself, amidst my reread of the Infernal Devices trilogy by Cassandra Clare (also for the millionth time); I want to write about elves in a young adult setting.

And boom, this was born.

The Heir to the Emerald Crown, to me, is born of all the things that I love about YA fantasy. It has drama, sassy characters, multiple points of view, trope-y scenes which bring me joy, and a pending romance that I cannot wait to dive into in book two. Yes, the title is on the books by me page. You're welcome.

And for my The Prince of Snow fans, you're welcome too.

There are many people I would like to thank along the way for this journey, specifically for Heir. I would like to firstly thank both of my editors. You never make me feel dumb for all of my misspellings and for that I am eternally grateful. And my cover designers, what I had pictured in my head was nothing like what you created. Thanks for reading my mind and making it better. Orlaith is gorgeous, and she has you to thank.

I would like to place emphasis on my author community for the utmost support. Without your encouragement from The Prince of Snow and The King of Flames, who knows if I would have felt it worth it to finish that thought one night while watching Lord of the Rings? (For the record, this book ended up being nothing like Lord of the Rings, but that's probably my favorite part of the whole thing. Orlaith most certainly could not handle an evil such as the ring of power. The emerald crown is bad enough for her.) ANYWAY, I would like to personally thank Nicole Platania and Chiara Gala for keeping my head on straight and my heart in the game. You guys are important to me.

Notable mentions also include Rowan Redfield, Imani Erriu, Christy R. Harrill, Marissa Serrao, and Jessica J. Ayala. You people are very important to me too.

Special thank you to my parents, who I forgot to announce to that I was writing this book to begin with. I announced it on social media; I figured that was enough.

To Will, thanks.

To my cats who sat with me to watch Lord of the Rings that one night (and every night), you are my gigas.

If you have managed to make it this far, I applaud you—and I promise that was the last time I am going to mention Lord of the Rings—but I also want to thank you, reader. Your dedication to me, my work, and my characters brings

ABOUT THE AUTHOR

L.B. Divine is a young adult fantasy author who drinks way too much coffee and spends too much time telling her cats how beautiful they are. She is constantly waking herself up from dreaming of Paris. She loves all stories, but fantasy ones are her favorite. The Prince of Snow is her first novel. She cannot wait to write all of the others that silently live in her brain. One day, she hopes to unleash them all upon you. L.B. Divine can be found at @lbdivineauthor on Instagram.